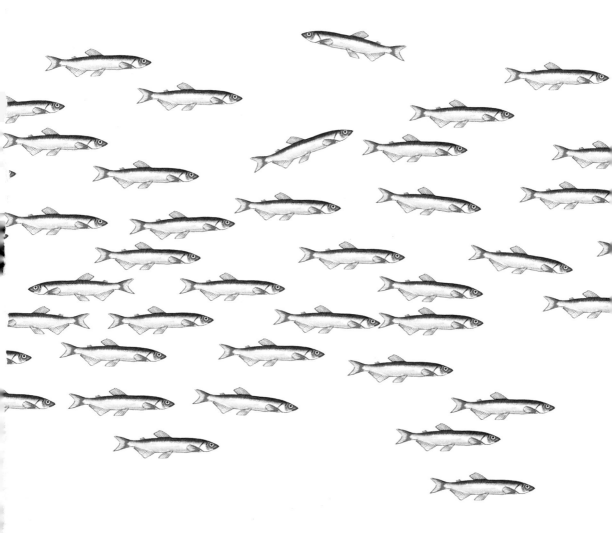

Published by Inhabit Media Inc.
www.inhabitmedia.com

Inhabit Media Inc. (Iqaluit) P.O. Box 11125, Iqaluit, Nunavut, X0A 1H0
(Toronto) 191 Eglinton Avenue East, Suite 301, Toronto, Ontario, M4P 1K1

English edition: The Man of the Moon
Editors: Neil Christopher and Grace Shaw
Designers: Astrid Arijanto and Sam Tse

Original title: Måenmanden
Published by milik publishing
Qaammatip Inua / Månemanden © Gunvor Bjerre, Miki Jacobsen & milik publishing,
2016
Design and layout copyright 2016 © milik publishing
Text copyright © 2016 Gunvor Bjerre
Illustrations by Miki Jacobsen © 2016 milik publishing
Designer: Ivalu Risager
Translator: Charlotte Barslund

We acknowledge the support of the Canada Council for the Arts for our publishing program.

This project was made possible in part by the Government of Canada.

Printed and bound in China by WKT Company Limited, March 2021, 20B2738

Canadä

Canada Council   Conseil des Arts
for the Arts   du Canada

Library and Archives Canada Cataloguing in Publication

Title: The man of the moon : and other stories from Greenland / retold by Gunvar Bjerre;
illustrated by Miki Jacobsen ; English translation by Charlotte Barslund.
Other titles: Måenmanden. English
Names: Bjerre, Gunvor, author. | Jacobsen, Miki, illustrator. | Barslund, Charlotte, translator.
Description: Translation of: Måenmanden.
Identifiers: Canadiana 20210121416 | ISBN 9781772272956 (hardcover)
Subjects: LCSH: Folklore—Greenland. | LCSH: Mythology, Greenlandic.
Classification: LCC GR214 .B4413 2021 | DDC 398.20998/2—dc23ww

THE MAN OF THE MOON

AND OTHER STORIES FROM GREENLAND

Retold by GUNVOR BJERRE
Illustrated by MIKI JACOBSEN
English translation by CHARLOTTE BARSLUND

INHABIT
MEDIA

CONTENTS

PREFACE

When the winter darkness had settled over Greenland for months on end and the frost had taken hold, people would pass the time on their sleeping benches in their small, low peat houses by telling old legends and myths that had been passed down through generations. The children would prick up their ears as they took in the stories, which they would one day tell to their own children.

Greenlandic legends and myths are often brutal, a testament to life on the edge of survival. They don't take place in a specific time; perhaps a thousand years ago, when people were made from stronger stuff than they are today.

Although children today can access stories from across the world via electronic media, oral tales can still compete with digital ones and capture children's imaginations.

In my selection I have prioritized stories about children and young people to help young readers identify with the protagonists.

As all myths and legends are based on oral traditions, there are often several versions of the same story, depending on how much the narrator has added or omitted—and, more importantly, remembered. I have chosen the versions I found most fascinating and vibrant.

This anthology is mainly based on *Myter og sagn fra Grønland* (*Myths and Legends from Greenland*) by Knud Rasmussen, volumes 1 to 4, selected by Jørn Riel (Forlaget Sesam, 2003). Jørn Riel has given permission for the stories to be based upon his version of Knud Rasmussen's original myths and legends.

I would like to thank Mariane Petersen, who has retranslated the stories into modern Greenlandic and has been an invaluable consultant along the way.

Gunvor Bjerre

Angakkuq

THE WHALE AND THE EAGLE THAT MARRIED TWO LITTLE GIRLS

Once upon a time, two little girls were playing house by the water's edge.

They built little houses from stones they found on the shore and pretended that small pieces of driftwood were their children.

However, they needed someone to play the father.

Suddenly, a shadow fell across their little stone houses. The girls looked up and saw a big, brown bird in the air. It was a white-tailed eagle.

"That can be the father. I'll marry it," one of the girls said.

The other girl also wanted a husband, so when she spotted a whale skeleton farther along the shore, she said:

"That can also be a father. I'll marry it."

If only they had never said those things.

As if it had heard her, the eagle pounced, sank its talons into the first girl, lifted her high up into the air, and flew off with her. It flew high up to a mountain ledge where it had its nest. There, it put her down.

The other little girl was terrified and started to cry, but before she had time to do anything, the whale skeleton turned into a real, living whale with skin and a body. It grabbed her and swam out to sea, to a small island where it put her in a cave.

Back home at their settlement, no one could understand why the two little girls didn't come home when it started to grow dark.

Their mothers ran down to the shore, calling out for them, but all they found were the little stone houses and some pieces of driftwood. They grew very worried and searched all over until late into the night, but there was no trace of the two little girls.

The mothers had no choice but to go home, still very upset, and wait for daylight.

They searched high and low for days. Everyone from the settlement joined in. One morning the mother of one of the girls noticed a big whale near a small island not far from the shore. She thought she could see something that looked like the trousers her daughter had been wearing.

A big *umiaq* boat was launched with the strongest men from the settlement onboard, and off they went, armed with harpoons and knives.

The little girl had cried until she could cry no more. The whale was lying in front of the cave, guarding it so she couldn't escape. It ordered her to pick lice, mites, and other pests from its skin.

While she was sitting there, staring across the water, she suddenly spotted something in the distance. Could it be true? Was it a boat with the men from her settlement coming to free her?

When the boat came closer, she realized she was right, but she acted as if nothing was happening so the whale wouldn't notice the boat.

But how would she ever get away from the big whale?

Then she had an idea.

"I need to pee," she said.

"You can pee into my mouth," the whale said.

"It's more than pee," she said.

"You can do that on my flipper," the whale said.

She didn't want to do that. She didn't like the thought.

"Very well. Off you go, then, and do your business, but be quick about it," the whale said.

The girl heaved a sigh of relief, but as she was about to leave, the whale grabbed her and tied a long strap to her wrist. It was clearly afraid that she would try to escape.

Once the girl was outside the cave, she took off the strap and tied it to a big rock.

"What's taking you so long?" the whale shouted impatiently, tugging at the strap.

"I'm coming, I'm coming," the girl shouted back. Then she bent down and in a soft voice asked the rock to repeat what she had just said should the whale ask again. The rock promised to do so.

"Hurry up," the whale shouted once more.

And this time the rock replied:

"I'm coming, I'm coming."

Meanwhile, the boat had reached the shore. The girl ran down to meet it and was helped on board by her father, who was thrilled to see his daughter again.

The men quickly got the boat back in the water and rowed so fast they left foam in their wake.

And then the whale discovered that it had been tricked. It rolled over in the water, creating a giant wave that nearly upended the boat.

The whale could swim faster than the men could row, so when it gained on them, the father called out to the girl:

"Throw your *kamiik* boots into the water."

The girl quickly pulled off her boots and threw them overboard.

When the whale saw the kamiik floating on the surface, it decided that the girl must have fallen into the water, so it stopped. But it soon discovered that it had been tricked and resumed its chase.

When it had nearly caught up with them again, the girl's father called out to her:

"Throw your fur into the water."

The girl quickly pulled her fur over her head, and even though she was cold, she threw it overboard.

Once again, the whale stopped, and the boat gained a small advantage.

But it was a brief respite, because the whale soon reached the stern of the boat again. The girl could see its eyes, which were bloodshot from rage, and it sent cascades of water over the fragile boat.

"Throw your trousers into the water," her father called out to her.

Shivering from cold, she managed to take off her skin trousers and throw them overboard to the whale.

It stopped yet again, and that gave the boat enough time to reach the shore by the settlement.

Kamiik

The girl, her father, and the other men ran as fast as they could up to the houses. Moments later they heard a loud noise.

They turned around and saw that instead of the whale there was now a giant whale skeleton at the water's edge, exactly where it had been on the day the girls were abducted.

Everyone was delighted that the girl was back safely. Yet there was one problem.

The girl asked where her friend was.

At first no one said anything.

"Where is she?" the girl said again.

"We don't know," someone said at last.

"I saw an eagle take her," the girl told them.

The moment she said it, all the men ran outside and looked up at the mountain where they knew the white-tailed eagle had its nest—and quite right! High up on a narrow ledge, they could see a tiny dot that could be a young child.

But they still couldn't help her because no one was able to climb up the vertical cliff face.

Her parents were miserable, and the rescued girl couldn't really enjoy her own freedom because her best friend was still a captive.

While one girl had been with the whale, the other had been sitting on the narrow ledge.

Every day the white-tailed eagle would go hunting, and every night it would bring home prey: lambs, caribou calves, hares, and fish.

Every time the girl got something to eat, she would save the long sinews from the meat, and whenever the eagle was away, she would plait them into a strap. With every passing day the line grew longer and longer, until one day the eagle noticed it.

"What are you doing with that?" it asked suspiciously.

"It's a hunting strap for you," the girl said, "to make it easier for you to catch your prey."

The eagle was reassured by her reply. It decided she had probably settled down and accepted her new life. It was wrong.

Once the strap was long enough, the girl waited for the eagle to fly off. Then she tied the strap to a protruding rock and started lowering herself down the cliff. It was difficult, and her hands hurt.

The strap was barely long enough, and she had to jump the last stretch to the ground.

She ran as fast as her legs could carry her and reached the settlement just as the eagle landed in its nest with a big salmon in its talons.

When it discovered that the girl was gone, it dropped the salmon and dived towards the settlement.

It landed on top of the house where she lived and started pecking a hole in the roof with its sharp beak in order to get inside and pull her out.

The girl sat inside the house listening to the scratching and bashing on the roof, while her brothers picked up their bows and arrows and went outside. They hid their weapons behind their backs.

They greeted the eagle politely and welcomed it.

"Seeing as you're now married to our sister," they said, "surely you're pleased to meet your new brothers-in-law. Why don't you spread your wings and greet us?"

The eagle suspected nothing, so it spread its big wings to greet the young men who were now its relations.

At that point, the brothers produced their bows and aimed their arrows right under the eagle's wings, so the arrows pierced its heart.

The eagle plummeted from the roof like a heavy lump. Stone dead.

There was joy at the settlement, and they held a feast that lasted several days.

The two little girls were delighted to see each other again, and the next time they played house, they didn't look for someone to play the father... and they were never getting married again.

THE GIRL WHO GOT LOST AND MET A FOX IN HUMAN FORM

Once upon a time, there was a mother and father who had a little daughter. Although there were other girls in the settlement, she nearly always played with the boys.

One day when she was out playing, she went with the boys deep into the mountains to play hide-and-seek. The girl found a good place to hide, but while she was waiting to be found, she began to feel very afraid of something. She didn't know what she was afraid of, but she climbed out of her hiding place and started wandering around.

She walked farther and farther away from the other children. She just kept on walking.

She ended up crossing the ice cap, and though she encountered many dangers along the way, nothing hurt her. She made it through all of them unscathed—until one day she reached a small settlement on the far eastern side of Greenland.

She was afraid to show herself to these people because she didn't know if they would welcome her, so she hid until it grew dark.

When everyone was asleep, she crept out and stole some food. She lived like this for a long time: hiding during the day and stealing food at night. For all that time she was on the east coast—and it was a long time—she never showed herself to anyone.

Many people in the settlement wondered who kept stealing their food, but they never found out.

And the strange thing was that during the time she was there, she didn't grow at all. She stayed a little girl.

One day she began to miss her parents and her old settlement very badly. So she started the long walk back, and just as on her outbound journey, she escaped all dangers.

When she was almost home, she began to feel faint from hunger. She hadn't eaten for a long time, and she was close to collapsing. Suddenly she saw a person, and when she got closer, she could see it

was a woman with her hair gathered at the top of her head in a huge
top knot.

When the woman saw her, she said:

"You look like you
could do with some-
thing to eat. Why
don't you come with
me to that small cave
over there? I have
lots of capelin."

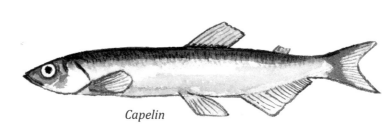

Capelin

The small, dried fish
were exactly what the little girl needed, and she was delighted to hear
there was food nearby.

She followed the woman to the small cave, and lo and behold, at the
back of the cave there was a big pile of dried fish. They climbed inside,
but as they tried to pick up the pile, they realized that a piece of string
was tied to it, and the moment they pulled the fish towards them, a big
rock fell down and blocked the entrance. It grew very dark inside the
cave. They realized they had climbed inside a fox trap, and the woman
suddenly turned into a fox.

The girl strangled the fox and took the fish. Then she waited for
someone to check on the fox trap. Meanwhile, she lived on fish and
fox meat.

After quite a while, she heard a man's voice say:

"I've trapped a fox at last."

But when he peeked through a small crack, he saw there was a
human inside the cave.

He got such a fright that he ran away. However, he soon came back
and had another look inside the cave. When the little girl just sat very
still and didn't say a word, he got scared and thought a spirit had crept
inside the trap.

He ran back to his settlement to fetch some men who could come
with him, just in case the little girl really was a spirit.

When the men approached the cave, she heard one of them say:

"Many years ago, we played hide-and-seek up here. A little girl went
missing and we never found any trace of her. It can't be her, can it?"

"You never can tell," another man said. "Let's have a look."

So they removed the rock from the entrance to the cave, and the little girl was free to crawl out into the light and open air.

Everyone was surprised to see her alive. They recognzed her easily because she hadn't grown in all the time she had been missing, but they had all assumed that she must be dead. The men were her old playmates. They were adults now, and the girl realized she must have been gone a very long time.

The girl told them about all her adventures, and the men told her what had happened in the settlement since her disappearance.

They told her that her mother was dead but that her father was alive and well.

Then she followed the men back to the settlement. The girl wanted to visit her father immediately, but he had gone hunting.

When he came back that evening with a seal tied to his *qajaq*, his kayak, the people shouted out to him from the shore:

"Your daughter is back!'"

The old man stopped paddling and said:

"If that's a joke, I think it's a very bad one."

"Come outside," the men called out to the little girl, and she emerged from her father's house where she had been waiting for him.

Her father recognized his little girl immediately, and even though he had aged a great deal, she also recognized him.

He paddled ashore as fast as he could. There was much joy when father and daughter hugged each other once more.

It was a comfort to the father, who was grieving the death of his wife. He had never thought for one moment that he would get to see his daughter again. He was convinced that she must have died a long time ago.

The girl moved back into her father's house, but she never grew up. For the rest of her life, she continued to look like the little girl who had once gone missing.

THE OLD MAN WHO TRAPPED CHILDREN INSIDE A ROCK

Once upon a time, an old man went out to hunt seal. He waited in his qajaq not far from the shore for some seals to swim by.

Finally, he saw a pod of seals poke their heads out of the water. He carefully paddled closer to them while trying to angle his qajaq so the seals wouldn't notice him. Every time they dived below the surface, he would quickly paddle towards the place he thought they would come back up for air. But every time he got it wrong, and the seals emerged quite a distance from where he was. And every time, he had to paddle faster to the next place where he reckoned they would be. At the same time, he had to take care that they wouldn't notice him. At last, he came quite close to them.

On the shore, some children were playing on the flat rocks that led straight into the water.

One of the children spotted the old man and said to the others:

"Look at that old man out there. Why don't we tease him by making the seals swim away?"

The other children agreed, and they started shouting as loud as they could:

"Hello, old man. Your trousers have patches on your bottom. Did you sew them on yourself?"

They shouted just as he was about to harpoon a big seal. The noise they made scared the seal off, and it dived below the surface as quick as lightning.

The children roared with laughter, but the old man was furious, and he ordered at the top of his voice:

"Rock, fold! Rock, fold!"

And the flat rock the children were standing on began to fold up around them. They tried to grab the youngest children and run away, but the rock enveloped them, and they couldn't escape through the cracks.

That satisfied the old man, and as there were no more seals to be caught, he paddled home.

Back at the settlement, the parents couldn't understand what was keeping their children, and they went down to the shore to look for them. They could hear their children's voices but couldn't see them anywhere. Then someone noticed that the rock had a new shape—and it sounded as if the voices were coming from inside it. And quite right: the children were crying and shouting through the cracks in the rock, but it was impossible for them to get out. Their parents couldn't get them out either.

Every day, the parents had to walk down to the rock with food. They would lower down seal blubber and mussel shells with seal soup to their children through the cracks in the rock, but they were miserable that they couldn't comfort their crying children.

Finally, they discovered that it was the old man's curse that had trapped the children, and they went to him to ask him to lift it. They promised him presents if he would do so.

The old man then walked up to the rock and said:

"Rock, unfold. Rock, unfold."

As soon as he had said the words, the rock began to open and assume the shape it had been when he first spoke his curse.

The children were free at last, but they were skinny and wretched to look at after being inside the rock for so long.

This was their punishment for teasing the old man. The old man was given many presents by the parents for setting the children free.

THE BEARS THAT CAUGHT BELUGAS

There once was a man who had a son he loved very much.

One day the boy fell ill, with a rash all over his body. The father had no idea what to do about it or how he could help his son.

So, he walked inland, hoping to find something that might cure his child.

He reached a small river, where he was lucky enough to catch a salmon. He brought the salmon back, hoping that somehow it would help.

When he came home, he let the tongue of the salmon touch the boy's rash—and all the boy's spots and sores disappeared, as if by a miracle.

The boy recovered and grew up to be a strong and brave young man.

One winter, the cold was especially severe. The sea was covered with thick ice, which made it almost impossible to catch anything. The people in the settlement were beginning to starve. Most hunters had given up going out to hunt, but the young man went out every day to see if he might be lucky enough to catch something.

One day, when the sun was shining very bright, he walked to the top of a mountain. There he sat down and looked across the icy sea.

Suddenly, he saw something in the distance that looked like the blow spray that comes out when a whale surfaces and breathes through its blowhole. It meant that there might be an opening in the ice, a stretch of open water where the whales could come up for air.

He hurried home to his father to tell him this news, and the next day he got up very early to make his way to the hole in the ice. When he arrived, he realized he wasn't the only person to have discovered the

stretch of clear water. Three big men were busy catching belugas. Each of them had caught a very big whale. The young man managed to catch a somewhat smaller whale.

The men asked him if he would like to come to their home to visit them. However, the young man knew that the people from his settlement were starving, so he decided to hurry back with his catch. He promised to visit them another time.

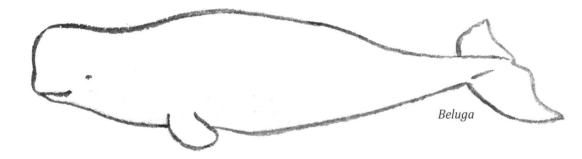

Beluga

It was true that people in his settlement were starving, but he was also a little scared of the big men. Besides, it sounded as if their home was a long way away.

The men slung the heavy whales over their shoulders as if they weighed nothing at all and walked away from the hole in the ice, taking long strides.

The young man dragged his small whale home with great difficulty, and by the time he got back, it had already grown dark. Everyone was overjoyed that he had come back with food, and it didn't take long to eat the small whale.

The young man told his father about the three men and their invitation to visit them. His father thought that he shouldn't go. You never could tell what kind of people they might turn out to be.

But the young man had nothing else to do, so instead of just sitting at home twiddling his thumbs, he decided to go back to the hole in the ice.

The next morning he woke up early, and when he reached the stretch of clear water, he saw that the three men were already busy hunting. Two of them had each caught a whale already, and the third was just about to. The young man carefully watched how the third man did it. A big male beluga surfaced, blowing mightily into the air. The third man pounced on it and followed it into the water when it dived back down.

It took such a long time before he reappeared that the young man was sure the man must have drowned. But suddenly he shot up to the surface with an enormous dead white whale in tow.

The young man also caught a whale with his harpoon. The three men asked him again if he would like to come home with them, but again he declined. He would rather wait until the next day, and then he would come only to visit them, not to catch whales.

When the young man came home, he told his father that he intended to visit the big men the next day. His father was worried, but he couldn't stop his son from doing so.

When the young man went out to the water the next day, the men were busy hunting. He watched them jump into the sea along with the whales, not resurfacing until they had killed them.

Yet again they asked if he would like to visit them, and this time the young man had no excuses, so he said yes.

They started walking towards the men's house. The young man didn't dare walk in front of them in case they decided to ambush him from behind, but they walked so quickly and their strides were so long that he struggled to keep up. The closer they got to their house, the faster they walked. The young man had to run to keep up because the men were walking so fast that the whales they were dragging behind them hardly even touched the ground.

The house was so far away that they didn't reach it until it was dark.

The men went inside the house with the whales, but the young man stayed outside for a moment to catch his breath—and also because he was a little apprehensive about entering.

When he finally pulled himself together and stepped inside, they had already eaten the three whales. Only the heads and a little of the necks were left.

Apart from the three big men, there were also their two old parents inside the house. They were so old that their faces were completely white.

"Oh, what a shame we don't have any fresh meat for our guest," they said.

So they found something else to give him, and when everyone had eaten, they started telling stories about their adventures.

The big men boasted about their strength, and the young man thought that it would be wise to get along with them. He regretted going with them, and he didn't feel very comfortable. He wouldn't stand a chance against the strong men if they decided to attack him.

Suddenly, the men's father suggested that his three sons should test their strength against the young man.

The young man got very scared, and before he knew it, the men had lowered a net from the ceiling, into which they threw the young man. They pushed the net back and forth between them like a swing. The young man nearly smashed his head against the roof because they pushed him so hard. He could see that the men were getting ready to pounce. He managed to jump out of the net and onto the floor.

The men loomed over him menacingly, and the young man had nearly died of fright when suddenly one of them said:

"Our parents gave us some amulets when we were little so we could take on all kinds of prey. Our amulets are little prawns. What's yours?"

Now, the young man didn't have an amulet, but he racked his brain. Then he remembered the rash he'd had all over his body when he was little.

"A small salmon was my amulet," he said.

Then the old father intervened. He said that a salmon—even a small one—had more power than a prawn, so he warned his sons not to test their strength against the young man. They wouldn't be able to beat him, given how strong his amulet was.

The young man breathed a sigh of relief, yet he was too scared to drop his guard completely.

When they went to bed that night, he stayed awake until everyone else was fast asleep. Then he slipped out of the house, and though it was pitch black outside, he ran as fast as he could.

Soon he could hear that someone was chasing after him. He glanced over his shoulder and saw two polar bears so old they were completely bald around their ears. He realized he couldn't outrun them, so instead of continuing towards the hole in the ice, he veered off and took a shortcut directly to his settlement.

The polar bears didn't notice what he did because it was so dark, and so he got away from them. When he got home, he told his father about his experiences, and they realized that he had visited bears in human form.

And so it happened that the salmon, which had once saved him from his rash, also saved his life.

KAASSASSUK THE ORPHAN

Once upon a time, there was a tiny boy whose name was Kaassassuk. Both his parents were dead, so he needed others to look after him. Several people in the settlement tried to care for him, but they quickly gave up. Finally an old woman took pity on him and said that he could live with her.

However, people looked down on the old woman, and she wasn't allowed to live with the others in the house itself, but had to sleep in the cooking station in the cold entrance tunnel to the house. So this is where Kaassassuk ended up living with her.

For some reason Kaassassuk didn't grow. The only things that did get bigger on him were his nostrils. Every day at dinnertime he would stand by the entrance to the common room to get some food. Everyone who lived in the house thought it was fun to tease the small boy, so when he stood there waiting, they would come along and lift him up by his nostrils. This made Kaassassuk's nostrils bigger and bigger.

But it didn't stop there. Whenever he had eaten a small, measly piece of meat and tried to help himself to another one, the men would pounce on him and say:

"How quickly he eats! We had better check to see if he has grown a tooth."

And they would pull a tooth out of the poor boy's mouth. He soon had no teeth to eat with, so he had to pull and tear at the meat with his toothless gums.

Fortunately, an old man felt sorry for the poor orphaned boy. He lent him his knife so Kaassassuk could cut the meat into small pieces.

The children in the settlement saw how the adults treated Kaassassuk, but they were still cruel to him.

Every time Kaassassuk came out to play, they would pounce on him and tease him about his size and his big nostrils. They would bully him and torment him, and the girls were just as bad as the boys.

So while the boys played outside with small toy harpoons, which their fathers had made for them, Kaassassuk had to hide with his

foster mother in the entrance tunnel to the house.

Although he was safe there, he was still itching to go outside and play with the others.

His friend who had lent him the knife noticed this and carved a tiny harpoon for Kaassassuk so he could join in the game. But he could have saved himself the trouble, because the moment Kaassassuk appeared with his harpoon, the big boys snatched it from him and broke it into lots of little pieces.

One day when Kaassassuk's friend, the old man, saw how the other children were teasing the poor boy, he walked up to him and said:

"Listen, my friend. You can't let them treat you like that. If you have the strength, I think you should walk to Talorsuit, behind the gorge. When you get there, you need to shout as loud as you possibly can, 'Lord of power. Here I am. Come to me.' And if the lord of power comes to you, then you must promise me not to be scared."

When Kaassassuk came home, he could think only of what the old man had told him.

As soon as he woke up the next morning, he got ready to leave. The old woman he lived with couldn't understand what he was up to—why he dressed himself in his warmest clothing and why he packed some food in a bag.

But Kaassassuk didn't tell her anything about his plans. When he appeared outside the house, he tried to sneak towards the gorge without being seen, but of course the other children noticed him.

They attacked him as usual, the girls and the boys. They teased him, called him names, threw him into the snow, and stuffed his mouth and nostrils with dirt and rubbish so he nearly choked.

When they finally let him go, he was filled with a strange sense of joy. Possibly because he knew there would soon be an end to all the teasing and tormenting.

He stuck a finger down his throat to throw up all the dirt and rubbish and cleared out his nostrils so he could breathe again.

Then he continued farther inland towards the gorge in the direction the old man had told him to go.

He tested his strength along the way, but he wasn't terribly successful. He tried to pull up some willow saplings out of the ground, but he couldn't. He tried picking up some small stones, but he couldn't manage that either.

Finally, he reached Talorsuit. Without pausing, he faced east and shouted at the top of his voice:

"Lord of power, here I am! Come to me!"

As he shouted, he heard a violent sound. The sound came closer and closer, and he saw a giant beast that looked like a dog. But it wasn't a dog. The beast floated in the air in front of him, and Kaassassuk could see that it had a human face and the body of an animal.

When the beast was very close to him, it said in a deep human voice:

"It has been a long time since anyone has summoned me. Wrap my tail around you, then I will fling you away."

Kaassassuk was trembling with fear. After all, he was only a tiny boy, and the creature was enormous. But he braced himself, wrapped its long tail around himself, and held on tight.

When he was ready, the beast flicked its tail violently, hurling Kaassassuk far away, and he rolled across the ground like a ball when he landed.

He staggered to his feet with great effort, groaning at the rough treatment. Then he heard the beast thunder in its powerful voice:

"Now look behind you."

Kaassassuk turned around and saw lots of toys scattered across the snow. They had been shaken out of him.

"All these toys are stopping you from growing," the beast said. "Now wrap yourself in my tail again."

Kaassassuk did as the beast told him to, and again he was sent flying with enormous force.

This time he hardened himself, so he only did a few somersaults before he managed to get back on his feet. He turned around, and this time he saw fewer toys lying in the snow.

"Come back tomorrow and summon me again," the beast said.

Then it disappeared across the sky towards the east, and Kaassassuk headed back towards his settlement.

Walking back seemed much easier than his outbound journey. He felt relieved and happy as he walked, and when he tried to pull up some willow saplings, they came up easily. He could even pull up thick willow trunks without any difficulties with just the one hand. And he could easily pick up the stones.

When he approached the settlement, he looked to see if he could sneak into the house without anyone noticing, but as usual the place was teeming with playing children.

And when they spotted Kaassassuk, they attacked him as usual, pulling his hair, scratching his face, and kicking him when he was down.

Although he felt much stronger, he acted as if nothing had changed and let them abuse him without fighting back.

The next day he walked back to the gorge and summoned the lord of power again, and the spirit did exactly what it had done the day before. But when Kaassassuk was sent flying this time, he did even fewer somersaults before he was back on his feet. And only a few toys fell out.

When the beast threw him again he just wobbled a bit, but he stayed on his feet, and not a single toy was left behind.

"From now on, no one can hurt you," the beast said. "But don't go boasting about your strength. You mustn't show anyone how strong you are until there's a special occasion. This autumn the men from your settlement will find a huge piece of driftwood. Then you can show them how strong you are. And later, three polar bears will come to your settlement. They'll also give you a chance to show your strength. You don't need me anymore."

The creature disappeared into the eastern sky, and Kaassassuk walked home to his settlement. His body felt light and strong, as if he were floating across the ground. He kicked big stones as if they were footballs, and when he reached a rock with a crack in it, he grabbed it and pulled the rock apart.

But no sooner was he back at the settlement than he was attacked and beaten up as usual, and he had to try very hard not to fight back, even though he was now strong enough to do so.

And so, life in the settlement carried on. Everyone teased him, children and adults, and when he tried to eat, the men would still pull him up by his nostrils. He was still given the smallest piece of meat, and they continued to pull out his teeth so that he wouldn't eat too much.

One autumn day the men came paddling home in their *qajait* with a huge driftwood trunk. As no trees grew near the settlement, everyone was delighted to get such a big piece of wood because now they had material for *umiat*, qajait, roof beams, and much more.

But the trunk was so big and heavy that no one could do anything other than secure it with long hunting straps. The plan was to spend all the next day dragging it ashore and cutting it up.

When everyone in the settlement was fast asleep, Kaassassuk snuck down to the sea. The driftwood trunk was still sloshing around at the water's edge. Kaassassuk grabbed hold of the hunting straps, but he was so strong that they snapped as if they were thread.

He pulled the trunk out of the water, and when it was safely ashore, he threw it over his shoulder and walked with it effortlessly. It was so heavy that he left deep footprints everywhere he walked, as if he had been walking in deep snow.

He carried the tree trunk up behind the house and planted it vertically in the ground. Then he quietly returned to his bench and quickly fell asleep. Soon afterwards he was woken up by a huge crash. The tree trunk had fallen over.

The next morning there was a huge commotion in the settlement. The men discovered that the driftwood trunk was no longer tied to the hunting straps. They were convinced that it must have drifted out to sea, but the sea was dead calm and no wind was stirring. What a mystery!

But then someone spotted the trunk behind the house, and everybody ran to see it. No one could understand who could possibly have dragged the heavy trunk up there. And whose footprints were those?

People looked at one another, and then they looked at the biggest and strongest man in the settlement.

"Did you do it?" they asked first him, then the other men, but no one would take the credit for the superhuman feat of dragging the trunk all the way up there.

Kaassassuk said nothing, and no one would think of asking him in their wildest dreams.

Eventually the people gave up on finding out, and started cutting up the driftwood instead and sharing it among them.

The fathers made toy harpoons for their sons out of the splinters and wood chips that were left over when the tree had been cut up, and as usual, no one thought about Kaassassuk. He looked enviously at the harpoons the other children were running around playing with, wishing he had a father who could make one for him. At last his friend, the old man, began to feel sorry for him and made him a fine toy harpoon.

But as usual the other children attacked him and snapped his harpoon in half and trampled on the pieces.

Then winter arrived, and it grew cold. The sea froze over, as did the breathing holes for the seals.

One morning they heard shouting outside. Kaassassuk and his foster mother had both been asleep, but Kaassassuk awoke and heard that people were talking about three polar bears on an iceberg outside the settlement. He understood that the time had come for him to show the people in his settlement that he wasn't the pathetic, feeble boy everyone thought he was. These had to be the bears that the lord of power had talked about.

Everyone who lived in the house got ready to go bear hunting, but it wasn't until they had all left the house that Kaassassuk asked his foster mother if he could please go look at the bears. She said yes, although she was somewhat surprised. Kaassassuk asked if he could borrow her kamiik because he didn't have a pair of his own. His foster mother was still half asleep, but she pulled off her kamiik and tossed them to him.

"But in return, you must get me two bearskins, one to lie on and one I can cover myself with," she said in jest.

Kaassassuk put on the far-too-big kamiik and tied them around his skinny legs with straps. Then he hurried out the entrance tunnel while his foster mother watched him, thinking she had never seen him so keen and excited before.

When Kaassassuk came outside, the men were all watching the three big bears that were still on the iceberg. No one dared to be the first to approach them, and every time one of the bears growled angrily, the men would retreat in fear.

When they saw Kaassassuk wearing the oversized kamiik and making his way to the iceberg, they started to mock him:

"Oh look, it's the big bear hunter. Have you lost your mind, Kaassassuk?"

But Kaassassuk hadn't lost his mind. He stood for a long time staring at the big bears, feeling powerful and brave. He had been looking forward to showing these cowardly people how strong he had become. Finally, they would know who they were dealing with.

And then he ran. Right at the group of men. They quickly stepped aside while they stared at the little boy with the too-big kamiik who fearlessly continued towards the iceberg. With his bare fists he punched the ice, creating a series of steps he could climb.

The moment he reached the top, the huge male bear went for him, raising its big paw to kill him. But Kaassassuk simply turned his back on it and hardened himself, just as he had done when he was hurled into the air by the lord of power.

The bear roared and landed a blow on Kaassassuk that would have killed anyone else, but Kaassassuk stayed where he was. He spun around, grabbed the bear's hind legs, and slammed it so hard against the ice that it broke its back and died.

Then the female bear attacked him, but Kaassassuk also turned his back on her as he had done with the male bear. When the blow hit him, he didn't hesitate for a moment, but spun around and grabbed the female bear by its hind legs and smashed it against the ice, killing it instantly.

The third bear was just a cub, but like its parents had done, it too attacked Kaassassuk. He grabbed it by one of its hind legs and swung it around his head before throwing it down right in front of the crowd of gawking men who couldn't believe their own eyes.

"This is your share of the catch," he called out to them.

The cub was killed the moment it hit the ice, and the men started skinning it immediately.

Then Kaassassuk took the two big bears he had killed, one in each hand, and as he ran he held them high over his head so they only occasionally touched the ground.

Oh, how he had longed for this moment when he could show them his enormous strength.

All his enemies, everyone who had teased and abused him, now came over to slap his shoulder, praise him, and ingratiate themselves with him.

"Dear Kaassassuk," they said, "save your strength and look after yourself. Would you like us to carry the bears for you?"

Kaassassuk didn't say one word to them and pretended not to hear them. He carried the bears up to the house and dropped them outside the entrance tunnel. Then he went to his old foster mother and said:

"Thank you for lending me your kamiik. I brought the two bearskins you asked me to get you, one for you to lie on and one to cover yourself with."

His foster mother was so surprised she couldn't say anything at all. She thought she must have misheard until she went outside with her skinning knife and saw the two big bears in front of the house. She still didn't say anything while she skinned the two big animals.

After she had skinned them, she cut the meat into big pieces. The rib meat is the tastiest on a bear, and the people would eat it when they had something to celebrate. As soon as she had cut out the big ribs, they were put into a pot and boiled. Then they were placed on large wooden dishes and everyone in the house gathered, looking forward to a great feast.

Everyone except Kaassassuk.

Where could he be? Then someone noticed him. He was in his usual place at the entrance to the common room, waiting for someone to pull him up by his nostrils.

The men looked at one another, rather embarrassed. They didn't know what to do. Then Kaassassuk's friend, the old man, said:

"What's wrong? Is no one willing to pick up Kaassassuk so he can have some food?"

Then he went over and stuck his fingers into Kaassassuk's nostrils and dragged him inside.

Kaassassuk took his usual spot by the window, but then all his tormentors, everyone who had beaten and kicked and abused him, called out:

"But dear, sweet Kaassassuk, you don't have to sit over there all alone by the window. It's way too cold. Come join the rest of us where it's warm."

But again Kaassassuk pretended not to hear them. No one knew what to do. And as it was Kaassassuk who had killed the bears, he had to be the first to eat.

They put out some knives so he could pick one and cut himself a big chunk of tasty meat.

But Kaassassuk ignored their knives. He took his old friend's knife and cut himself a tiny piece of rib meat, as usual, and started gnawing it. This was the signal that the others could now eat, and they threw themselves at the big, delicious chunks of meat.

When Kaassassuk had eaten the meat on the rib, he cut himself another one and said:

"Today I'll eat a lot because I have a knife to help me eat."

Then all the men said in flattering voices:

"Eat as much as you like, you deserve it. But mind you don't choke."

Everyone wanted to be his friend now because he was so big and strong.

When Kaassassuk had eaten his meat, he looked at the water bucket.

"It would be nice to have some water now," he said.

"Of course," the others said, "but this water isn't good enough for you. Let us get you some fresh, cold water."

And they sent two girls out to get fresh water for him. They were as quick as they could be and soon returned with a small bucket of lovely, ice-cold water.

Kaassassuk took a small sip.

Then he decided that the time had come to take revenge on all his tormentors, everyone who had teased and abused him and made his life a living hell.

"Come over here," he said to one of the girls who had helped torment him.

The girl went over to him, and he pretended to give her a hug to thank her for fetching water. But when he put his arm around her, he squeezed her so tight that she dropped down dead.

Then he grabbed one person after the other and squashed them all to death.

People were terrified and tried to get out of the house, but Kaassassuk blocked their path. He saw that the old man and his wife and also his foster mother were frightened and trying to get out, but he said to them:

"You have been good to me and helped me. You have nothing to fear."

Finally, he had taken his revenge and killed everyone in the settlement. The only three people left alive were the ones who had been good to him.

Now that all the other hunters in the settlement were dead, there were lots of qajait lying around unused.

One day he said to the old man:

"I would like to learn how to paddle a qajaq."

Together they walked down to the shore to pick out a qajaq that would be suitable for him.

To begin with, Kaassassuk paddled close to the shore, but when the weather was fine, he ventured farther out, and it wasn't long before he was a skilled qajaq paddler.

Now he was able to go hunting in a qajaq and provide food for himself and the three old people in the settlement.

At times, he would go on longer trips up and down the coast, but no matter where he went, people were scared of him. The rumour of his enormous strength and everything he had done had spread along the whole coast.

One day he heard about a man who was so strong that no one had managed to beat him. This man's name was Ususaarmiarsunnguaq. This intrigued Kaassassuk because he wanted to be stronger than anybody else.

When the ice broke up and it was possible to sail on the sea again, he told the old people in the settlement that he wanted to go north to do battle against Ususaarmiarsunnguaq.

After travelling for several days, he reached the settlement where the strong man lived. He went ashore and told some men who were chatting that he would like to meet Ususaarmiarsunnguaq and fight him.

The men looked at one another, then pointed to a tiny man who didn't look very impressive.

Kaassassuk thought it would be easy to beat such a small man, so he went over to him and asked if he wanted to fight.

Ususaarmiarsunnguaq spent a long time looking Kaassassuk with the big nostrils up and down. Then he said they could meet the next morning.

Kaassassuk could barely sleep that night because he was so excited about the fight, which he was sure he would win.

When he woke up the next morning, he saw that Ususaarmiarsunnguaq was already waiting for him. He was standing at the shore of a lake, and all the local people had come to watch the fight.

The two men began fighting. Kaassassuk was sure he could easily win, but he was proven wrong. Firstly, Ususaarmiarsunnguaq was much stronger than he looked. Secondly, he was as slippery as a fish and kept slipping out of Kaassassuk's arms every time he tried to squash him.

The battle went back and forth all day. When the sun began to set, people shouted that they had to hurry up and finish because it was getting dark. Then Ususaarmiarsunnguaq employed all his strength. Quick as a flash he grabbed Kaassassuk, held him up in the air in his outstretched arms, and threw him into the lake, where he made a huge splash as he landed.

When Kaassassuk surfaced, drenched and covered in plants from the bottom of the lake, all the men laughed with derision.

He was so embarrassed that he slunk into his tent without looking at anyone, and the next morning he left before dawn so he would not run into any of the local people.

Since that day, Kaassassuk never challenged anyone again, nor did he boast about how strong he was.

ANARTEQ, WHO TURNED INTO A SALMON

Once upon a time, there was an old man who had one son and many daughters. The son's name was Anarteq, and he was a skilled hunter. Now that his father had grown old, Anarteq was the one who went hunting for food for the family.

The whole family would go caribou hunting at the bottom of the fjord. Once they got there, the sisters would drive the caribou into a lake where Anarteq would be waiting in his qajaq, ready to kill them.

One day when they were hunting caribou in the fjord as usual, the girls were chasing the caribou into the lake and Anarteq was busy killing them.

Then a caribou calf swam very close to his qajaq. He grabbed its tail and played with it for a while when it suddenly kicked out and upended the qajaq. Anarteq tried to climb back inside it, but the qajaq filled with water, and he had no choice but to abandon it.

On the shore his sisters watched him struggle. They were worried because Anarteq didn't know how to swim, and they were distraught that they couldn't help him.

Suddenly Anarteq called out from the lake:

"The salmon have started to eat my legs!" And he slowly sank to the bottom, losing consciousness.

When Anarteq came around, he discovered that he had turned into a salmon.

The father and the rest of the family sailed home to their settlement, and the father now had to go hunting again like he used to when he was younger. But he had no wish to go to the bottom of the fjord to hunt caribou any longer.

Once Anarteq had turned into a salmon, he would swim with the other salmon into the sea to grow fat before returning to the lake every year when the ice broke up.

Several years later his father decided to hunt caribou again. Along with his daughters, he rowed into the fjord. It was very difficult for him. The trip reminded him so much of his son that he started to weep.

As they were rowing the umiaq, Anarteq and a big run of salmon came swimming down the fjord on their way to the lake. When Anarteq saw the umiaq with his father and his sisters, he swam up to them and nibbled the father's steering oar.

The father grew scared, quickly withdrew the oar, and said:

"I wonder if that was Anarteq."

At that the sisters started to cry. They too missed their brother.

When the father put the steering oar back in the water, Anarteq bit it hard. This time his father slowly pulled up the oar so that Anarteq came with it.

Once Anarteq surfaced, he was transformed back into a man. His father and his sisters were overjoyed, and Anarteq hunted for food for his family for many years.

THE WITCH WHO ABDUCTED CHILDREN IN HER AMAUTI

Once upon a time, there was a man and his wife who desperately wanted another child. Now, they did have a daughter who was almost an adult, but they very much wanted another baby.

One day the wife discovered she was expecting a child, and some time later she gave birth to a little girl.

The parents were delighted with their new baby and did everything they could to make sure she was happy, and so they couldn't understand why their little girl would cry every night. She cried and she cried and she cried—she cried so much that she couldn't fall asleep.

The father asked his older daughter to look after the little girl and see if she could make her stop crying and get her to fall asleep.

The older girl walked around with her sister in her arms, rocking her and singing to her, and finally the child fell asleep.

But the older girl had many other duties to attend to around the house, so while the baby was asleep, she started her chores. When she finished them, she decided to check up on her sister, but discovered to her horror that the baby wasn't where she had left her.

She searched both inside and out, but couldn't find her baby sister anywhere. Finally, she had to wake her parents and tell them.

They were both horrified and upset, and the father was angry with his older daughter for not taking better care of her sister.

He was so angry that he wanted to kill her, but fortunately her mother talked him out of it. After all, the older daughter couldn't help what had happened, and losing one daughter was bad enough.

The older daughter offered to go see a great shaman who lived in the south and ask him for help trying to find her sister.

So she got up very early the next morning and walked as fast as she could to the shaman's settlement. She explained what had happened to her family, and he promised to return with her to see if he could find out where the baby was.

When the shaman and the older daughter returned to the family's house, they were tired and hungry after their long trip. But the parents were very rude.

They didn't offer the shaman any food or anything to drink. All they were interested in was how soon he could contact his helper spirits.

The father in particular pestered him.

Although the shaman was as hungry as a bear, he started to prepare for the ritual. He covered the windows so no light could come in. It was easier for him to meet his helper spirits in the dark.

Then he started summoning his helper spirits. He tied ropes around his arms and legs and said spells, but nothing worked. He was unable to contact his helper spirits, so they couldn't tell him where the little girl was.

The father grew furious with the shaman, and even though it was the middle of the night, he chased him out of the house. Tired and hungry, the shaman had to find his way home in pitch-black darkness.

When he returned to his own settlement, he told the people there of his experiences and the bad treatment he had been subjected to.

The people were outraged at the way he was treated and they suggested that if the family came back wanting help again, the shaman shouldn't go himself, but should send the bachelor instead.

This bachelor was something of a wretch. His hips were lame, so he could only walk by supporting himself on his crutches.

The next day the missing girl's father came to the shaman's settlement. He wanted to ask the shaman for help again, but just as he reached the settlement, the bachelor happened to emerge from his tent.

The people pointed to him and said to the father:

"If you're looking for a really great shaman, then ask that man over there."

The father went up to the bachelor and asked if he could help.

Now, the bachelor was indeed a shaman, but he wasn't used to people talking to him or wanting his help, so he was delighted to be asked. For that reason, he walked with the father back to his settlement.

The parents didn't appear to have learned anything from the last shaman's visit because they treated the bachelor in the exact same way: no food, nothing to drink, and they pestered him to start the ritual long before darkness.

Again, the windows were covered, all lamps were extinguished, and the bachelor started calling for his helper spirits even though he was tired, hungry, and thirsty.

This time was more successful. Not long after he started, the bachelor cried out:

"I know where your child is. Amaarsiniooq, the witch who lives up on the eastern *nunatak*, mountaintop, is keeping her in her *amauti*, the pouch at the back of her parka."

The family was delighted to hear this. The lamps were relit and the most delicious food was brought out: boiled seal, dried caribou meat, and many other delicacies.

"I think I'll go get her as soon as we've finished eating," the father said.

But the bachelor thought that was a very bad idea.

"If you go there on your own, you'll never be able to get your daughter back, but if I go up there, I think I'll succeed," he said.

When they went to bed that evening, the father told the bachelor that he was welcome to sleep with his older daughter. This made the bachelor happy because he had never slept with a woman before.

The next morning, they rose early and got ready to sail to the bottom of the fjord where the huge glacier met the sea.

The bachelor went ashore and said to the father:

"I want you to sail back to your settlement. And then pick me up here tomorrow at the same time."

And then he struggled on his poor legs up towards the glacier where he believed Amaarsiniooq the witch was living. It was slow going, but

Nunatak

40

eventually he saw a house that had light pouring out of it.

He crept nearer to it and tried to find a way in, but it seemed to have no entrance. Then he discovered a small air hole where the heat from the house was coming out.

He carefully climbed up and peered through the hole. He was relieved when he saw Amaarsiniooq sitting on a bench. A small baby was sleeping in her amauti.

But Amaarsiniooq herself wasn't asleep.

The bachelor waited for a long time for her to fall asleep, but it didn't look as if the witch was going to sleep. It was morning, after all.

I had better use my magic powers, the bachelor thought to himself, and began to sing a spell that usually made people fall asleep. But he couldn't be sure it would work on a witch.

After he had been singing for some time, he saw that the witch's eyelids were getting heavier, and she was starting to nod her head. Before she lay down on the bench, she removed the amauti, took out the little girl, and placed her by her side.

When he was sure Amaarsiniooq was fast asleep, the bachelor tried once again to find a way of getting inside the house—and this time he found an entrance.

He carefully crept through the entrance tunnel to the house, scared that the witch might wake up. To be on the safe side, he kept singing the spell. He nearly didn't succeed because the threshold to the house was so high that he could barely straddle it with his bad legs, but he finally made it inside.

He carefully lifted the baby, but the little girl woke up and was so frightened at seeing a total stranger that she started to cry.

"Shh, don't cry," he whispered. "Don't be scared of me. I'm here to bring you home to your parents."

And then he crawled back out of the house with the baby in his arms.

Once he was back outside, he used another spell so that rather than limp, he could rush down towards the fjord.

However, the baby's crying had woken up Amaarsiniooq. She turned into a falcon and flew after them.

Even though the bachelor had used a spell to help him move quickly, the falcon was swifter and soon caught up with them.

Amaarsiniooq turned into herself again. She grabbed both the baby and the bachelor, stuffed them into her spacious amauti, and tightened the strap at the top. Then she made her way back to her house high up on the glacier.

While the bachelor was lying in the darkness with the baby, he thought desperately about what he could do to save himself and the little girl, who was now wailing.

Then he remembered that he had a helper spirit who was good at throwing stones. He summoned the spirit, which soon came rushing from the ice cap. It hurled one big stone after the other at Amaarsiniooq, but no matter how hard they hit her, she just laughed out loud.

The bachelor grew desperate. He thought of all his helper spirits and decided to summon the one that was a falcon.

Moments later, the falcon came swooping, emitting its loud cry of "*cri, cri, cri, cri*." It made straight for the witch and attacked her with its beak and talons, but she simply carried on walking as if nothing had happened.

Eventually, however, she couldn't take any more—any more of the stones that kept raining down on her or any more of the scratching and pecking of the falcon. She ducked and dived in order to avoid the sharp talons, which loosened the strings on the amauti.

The bachelor seized his chance. He let the child slip out onto the ice and followed suit. Then he grabbed the child and rushed towards the fjord while the stone-thrower and falcon helper spirits dealt with the witch.

He reached the shore safe and sound, and there the little girl's father was waiting with his boat as they had agreed.

The bachelor gave the baby to the father and told him to sail quickly back to the settlement with her. He himself would follow shortly.

The father was delighted to have his little girl back again, as were the mother and the older sister, but they couldn't understand why the child kept crying. After all, she was home now and back with her family. Yet the baby was inconsolable.

The bachelor, who had also returned to the settlement, asked if they wanted him to find out why she cried all the time.

The parents were very grateful for everything the bachelor had done for them and happy to have their little girl back, but if the bachelor could also make her stop crying, they would be even more grateful.

He mumbled and sang and said strange spells. Suddenly he said:

"She cries because she has lost her soul. It's somewhere else completely. I'm going to fetch it for her."

Off he went, and later he returned with a small creature in his arms. The small creature was an exact copy of the little girl. He placed the soul next to the child, and slowly the little girl calmed down and stopped crying.

Later the parents looked in on the girl and her soul, and saw that they had merged together into one. The little girl had gotten her soul back. After that day she was always a happy little girl who never cried any more than children usually do.

"As a thank you for helping us so much," the father said to the bachelor, "you can marry our older daughter, and as you can't go hunting yourself because of your bad legs, I promise to make sure you'll never be short of meat."

He kept his promise. There was always meat in the pot in the bachelor's home.

And the bachelor himself? Well, he was delighted that he finally got himself a wife.

THE GREAT SWIMMER

A man and his wife lived in a small settlement on the coast. The wife was probably the only one who liked the man, because he was harsh and cruel and had no friends.

He did, however, have many enemies because of his aggressive nature and because he frightened everyone away by being brutal and rude towards them.

Indeed, he was so unpopular that hunters from nearby settlements had threatened to kill him. Every time he went hunting, his wife was scared that he might not return, but every evening she was relieved to see his qajaq pull up on the shore.

One day the man and his wife had a little boy. The man was ever so proud to have a son, and soon after the boy was born, he took the baby down to the sea. There he threw the little boy into the icy water.

"He must be toughened up," the man said as he quickly pulled the screaming child out of the water. He didn't do this to hurt the child. He just wanted his son to grow up strong so he would survive the tough environment.

Every day the father would throw the child into the water, and slowly the child became able to stay in the cold water for longer and longer. He even learned to swim and became a very good swimmer as he grew up.

One day when his father came back from hunting, he had a particularly big seal tied to the side of his qajaq.

The father asked the mother to skin the seal in a special way, and the skin was stretched out and hung up to dry.

Afterwards, the mother softened the skin by chewing it and made a seal suit for her son from it.

At this point the boy had grown tall, and when the suit was ready, the father gave it to him as a kind of swimming costume and said to him:

"Now I'm going to paddle out into the sea, and I want to see how long you can swim after me. Just keep swimming outwards. I'll follow you in the qajaq."

The seal suit made it possible for the boy to swim fast. He swam and he swam, much of the time underwater.

Once he had swum as far as he could, he started to turn around—but his father wasn't satisfied. The boy had to be toughened up even more, so the father threatened him with his harpoon and forced him to carry on swimming.

At last the father was happy. The son was allowed to turn around, and even though he was exhausted, he swam for a long time underwater on his way back to the shore. Indeed, he swam under the water for so long that his father got scared that he might have been too strict and that the boy had drowned.

But then he saw the boy's head surface close to the coast, and he breathed a sigh of relief.

He quickly sailed over to him and praised the boy. The truth was he was very proud of his son.

Now you might have thought that the father would stop there, but oh, no.

The boy had to be pushed even further.

"Show me once again how far you can swim," the father said, and chased the boy back into the water. And the boy, who was used to obeying his father, did as he was told even though he was close to collapsing from exhaustion.

He threw himself into the waves once more and dived under the surface in his seal suit.

The father paddled out in his qajaq, but started to worry when he couldn't see the boy.

I hope nothing has happened to him, he thought to himself. *I hope he hasn't drowned. I wonder if I went too far.*

But then he saw his son's head appear much farther out than he had expected. He quickly sailed to him and praised his son to the skies.

"Right, you can swim back now. I'll follow you in the qajaq, and this time don't dive under the water."

And the boy swam ashore using the last of his strength.

One morning the strict father went hunting in his qajaq, but he didn't return in the evening. The boy was standing by the shore scouting for him, but he never came.

Instead, a qajaq from a nearby settlement appeared. The boy invited the man ashore and asked if he had seen his father.

But the qajaq paddler refused to go ashore. Instead he said in a menacing voice:

"Today we got your father, tomorrow we'll come and kill the rest of your settlement."

Then he turned his qajaq around and paddled away.

The boy said nothing to his mother about what had happened. He didn't want to make her any more worried than she already was because his father hadn't come home.

The next day the boy saw some qajait approaching the settlement. He quickly put on his seal suit and ran down to the shore and out onto a small, protruding rock.

The men paddled their qajait towards him. As he stood there, he heard one of them say:

"He's just a boy. He should be easy to harpoon."

Just as they were about to throw a harpoon at him, he jumped into the icy sea.

The men were very confused.

"Did he just fall into the water?" one of them said.

They weren't used to people who could swim, and they certainly couldn't swim themselves.

They paddled their qajait to the spot where the boy had disappeared into the waves, but they couldn't see him.

The boy had dived into the water and quickly swum out to sea. When they spotted his head far away, they gave chase. And that was exactly what the boy had been hoping they would do. In that way he managed to coax them farther and farther away from the settlement.

Some distance into the open sea was a big iceberg. The boy swam to it and managed to pull himself up by his fingernails and strong fingers. He climbed to the top of the iceberg.

From there he could see the qajait approaching. He saw how his enemies carved steps into the ice so they could reach him. But when the first hunter's head appeared over the edge of the iceberg, the boy was ready. He pushed a big lump of ice right at the men and heard them scream as they fell into the icy water, where they drowned, because none of them knew how to swim.

There were still several men in the qajait at the foot of the iceberg. A few more tried to scale it, but they met with the same treatment and drowned in the sea.

Now the last of the men decided to turn around. It was too difficult and too dangerous to capture the boy.

They started paddling their qajait back to their own settlement.

But now it was the boy's turn to chase them. He jumped back into the water and swam after the qajait. The men didn't notice him, so they were shocked when he suddenly appeared alongside their qajait and pulled the paddles from them.

The qajait nearly keeled over, but the men managed to straighten them and tried desperately to paddle ashore using just their arms.

However, the furious boy refused to let them get away. He grabbed their arms one after the other and pulled them into the sea, where they drowned.

Finally, just one man was left.

When he saw the boy approach, he cried:

"I wish I had never gone with them. How will my old mother manage if I die?"

When the boy heard that, he was reminded of his own mother, who had only him to go hunting now that her husband, his father, had died.

"I'll let you live," he said to the hunter. "Now paddle back to your settlement and warn them that if anyone comes near our settlement again, they won't get out alive."

The man didn't need telling twice. He picked up one of the paddles floating on the water and paddled home as quickly as he possibly could.

Then the boy swam back to his own settlement and told them what had happened.

His mother was distraught at having lost her husband, but she was also very proud of her son.

For the next few days the people from the settlement kept a lookout. They thought perhaps someone would come and avenge all the dead men, but the boy appeared to have frightened off their enemies for good. No stranger ever dared to come near the settlement again as long as the great swimmer was alive.

THE CHILD SNATCHER

It is said that a big monster lives at the bottom of the sea. Its name is Qalutalissuaq. You often hear sounds coming from the sea where the monster is—sounds similar to the noise you make when you bail water from a boat. And Qalutalissuaq does indeed mean "the bailer."

It is also said that this monster likes to snatch children. Especially noisy, screaming children.

Once upon a time some children were playing on the shore. They were shouting to one another, as children tend to do when they play.

Suddenly Qalutalissuaq appeared, and the terrified children fled to the mountains—all except a small orphan boy whose kamiik had no soles, so he couldn't run as fast as the other children or jump across the rocks. When the monster caught him, he threw himself onto the ground and wiggled and kicked his legs.

His naked feet stuck out of his boots that had no soles. Although he was frightened, he stuck his toes right up into the monster's nose. He wiggled and waved his big toe and shouted:

"If I were you, I would be very scared of my big toe. Because it eats monsters and people!"

The monster got so scared that it left him alone and hurried back into the sea immediately—and no one has heard anything of Qalutalissuaq ever since.

THE WILD GEESE THAT MADE THE BLIND BOY SEE

Once upon a time, there were two children, a boy and a girl, who lived with their old grandmother. Their parents had died, and their grandmother looked after them, but she treated them badly.

The boy was the elder, and he had already started to go hunting to get food for the family.

One day he shot a fine, white bearded seal, and when he brought it back that evening his grandmother said:

"I think I'll make myself a pair of trousers from its skin."

White bearded seals were quite rare, so a pair of trousers like that would be something very special indeed.

When the boy heard that, he said he had planned to make straps out of the skin, which he could use for fishing, and ganglines for his dogsled. His grandmother got very annoyed. She had her heart set on a pair of fine, white fur trousers, but all she said was:

"Well, go ahead and make your straps then. I can always make myself a pair of trousers some other time."

And she started preparing the skin. She scraped off the blubber and removed the hair so the boy could cut his straps. But when she was nearly done, she whispered across the skin:

"Once he has cut his straps and begins to stretch them, I want you to snap. I want you to spring back, hit his eyes, and blind him."

The bewitched skin did as the evil grandmother had told it to. When the boy cut his straps and started stretching them, they snapped back right into his eyes and blinded him.

Now, being blind meant he could no

Bearded Seal

longer go hunting, so he was forced to stay at home.

During winter the boy grew increasingly sad. At the start of spring, his grandmother spotted a big bear heading towards their settlement. She ran to the blind boy and said:

"A big polar bear is coming. I know you can't see it, but if I help you aim your bow and arrow, you might be able to hit it. You're much stronger than I am."

The boy jumped up and went with her outside. The grandmother aimed the arrow and the bow, and the boy fired it. The bear let out a loud roar when the arrow hit its armpit and went straight through to its heart. It fell to the ground, dead.

"Oh, what a shame," the evil grandmother called out. "You missed it."

"How odd," the boy said. "I heard a noise that sounded exactly like a bear being shot in the heart."

His sister helped him back inside the house, and he sat down on the bench feeling very disappointed.

Then he heard his sister rummage around for something.

"What are you looking for?" he asked.

"Grandmother's skinning knife," she said.

"But why would she want that when I missed the bear?" the boy wondered out loud.

"I don't know," his sister replied. Her grandmother had given her strict instructions not to say anything about the bear to her brother.

The grandmother cut up the bear into many pieces and saved the meat for herself. She grew fat on the meat but never gave the boy anything—and his sister was only given small pieces every now and then. The girl felt sorry for her brother and saved half of what she was given under her clothes. She would pass it to him when their grandmother wasn't looking.

The boy, who had been used to roaming around the mountains and the ice, found it very difficult to be inside all the time, so one day he asked his sister to help him walk up a nearby mountain.

When they had reached the top, he said to her:

"I want you to go home and leave me here. You can come back for me in three days."

The boy enjoyed sitting outside in the fresh air and listening to the sounds of nature around him: birds singing, a fox baying, and the *whoosh* of bird wings whenever great flocks passed by.

Later that day six wild geese came flying. They landed on the mountaintop where the boy was sitting and said:

"Why do you look so sad?"

The boy told them he had been blinded by some straps that had snapped back into his eyes.

"The straps didn't blind you," the geese said. "Your evil grandmother did. She bewitched the skin so it snapped back into your eyes."

Now, as you would expect, the boy got angry and very sad to hear that.

The geese moved closer to him and said:

"We would like to help you. All you have to do is sit quite still and put up with whatever we do to you, even if it doesn't feel very nice."

One of the geese flew over him and a big bird dropping landed right in his eyes. The boy was startled, but the goose came back and wiped his eyes clean with its wings. The geese continued to fly over him and land bird droppings in his eyes. Big, warm, and wet splodges. His eyes stung and bird poo dribbled down his cheeks, but the birds wiped them clean as best they could with their feathers.

Suddenly, the boy thought things around him started to get brighter, but he still couldn't see anything clearly. Finally, the biggest gander flew over him. It released a dropping so big that the boy's face was completely covered. He gasped for breath and was close to tears because his eyes stung so badly. But when the gander came over and wiped his face with its wings, the boy could suddenly see just as well as he could before he was struck by the bewitched straps.

The boy was overjoyed and thanked the wild geese, and they continued their flight across the mountains.

After three days passed, his sister came to fetch him. He didn't say anything about the geese, but pretended he was still blind. His sister, however, wondered why he was walking more easily and faster on the way back and without tripping or stumbling. She decided it was probably the fresh air that had made him feel better.

When they returned to the settlement, he opened his eyes just a

little. He saw a fine, big polar bear skin on the stand that was normally used for drying meat, and when he was about to crawl into the house through the entrance tunnel, he saw the shoulder of a large bear right by the opening. Once inside the house, he carefully opened one eye without his grandmother noticing. He saw a big, lovely bear ham lying on a dish under the sleeping bench.

His grandmother hadn't noticed anything. She was merely mildly irritated that he was home again, but all she said was:

"Oh, so you're back, you wretch. How are your eyes?"

The boy replied that there was no change. Then he sat down on the bench and was silent for a long time. Finally he opened his mouth and said:

"I had a strange dream last night. I dreamt there was a big bear ham right under this bench. In my dream I also saw a polar bear skin out on the drying stand, and right next to the entrance was a giant bear shoulder."

The boy opened his eyes and looked right at his grandmother. He bent down and pointed to the ham under the bench.

"And here's the very thing I dreamt about."

His grandmother was shocked when she realized that the boy could see again. Now she had been found out. But his sister jumped for joy.

His grandmother then said in her sweetest voice:

"Oh, yes, that. That's the ham I've been saving so we could celebrate you coming back from the mountains."

But the boy was having none of it.

"No, thanks. I'm going out to catch some fresh food for myself," he said.

He took his harpoon and went outside to the sea. He loved being able to see again. At that very moment a pod of belugas swam past.

The boy threw his harpoon and hit one of the whales. With great effort he managed to haul it ashore using the hunting strap that was tied to the end of his harpoon.

His evil grandmother soon came running outside with her skinning knife. She called out:

"Let me help you cut it up."

"No," the orphan boy said. "This whale is for me, and I will share it only with my sister. But I don't mind helping you catch one for yourself. All you have to do is hold the hunting strap and pull it in."

The evil grandmother was happy to do so. After all, there is a lot of meat on a beluga. The boy had tied the strap firmly around her waist when suddenly she grew anxious.

"I hope you won't catch too big a whale for me."

"No, no. Don't you worry. I'll find you a small one," the boy said.

Together they walked out to a small headland from where they could see the belugas. They spotted a small one, and the grandmother said:

"Please catch that one for me."

The boy got ready to harpoon it—but at that moment a giant whale swam past.

The boy threw his harpoon at it instead, and the grandmother found a big stone to brace her feet against so she could reel in the whale with the strap.

The whale resisted and pulled hard on the strap, but the grandmother was strong. When it looked like she was going to be successful, the boy walked over and gave her a nudge. She slipped, lost her footing, and fell into the water with a splash. The whale tugged at the strap, and she disappeared under the surface. Every time the whale came up to breathe, the boy saw his grandmother's top knot pop up through the water. And every time he could see that she was gaining on the whale.

Then she surfaced and screamed at the top of her lungs:

"*Uluga, uluga, uluga*—my skinning knife, get me my skinning knife!"

Finally, she pulled herself all the way up onto the whale and was riding on its back while she screamed and shouted for her knife. But the boy didn't want to throw her the knife, so the whale swam off with the evil grandmother still on its back. Thus, she was punished for being mean to her grandchildren. No one has seen her since. And no one has missed her either.

QILLARSUAQ AND THE ORPHAN BOY

Qillarsuaq was known wide and far as a great hunter and shaman. Once upon a time, he went bear hunting with an orphan boy. They drove so far across the frozen sea on their sled that they couldn't see land anywhere.

Then a storm gathered. It was so powerful that it caused the sea ice to crack. Suddenly, Qillarsuaq and the orphan boy found themselves on an ice floe, unable to get back to the shore.

The storm drove them farther and farther into the open sea.

"Lie down on the sled and close your eyes," Qillarsuaq shouted over the storm. "If you open them, even once, then we're lost."

The boy did as he was told. He lay down on the sled, pressing his eyes tightly shut.

As he was lying there, he couldn't see anything, of course, but suddenly it felt as if the dogs and sled gained great speed. And as far as the boy could sense, they were heading towards the shore. He couldn't understand how that was possible, because there were no ice floes connecting them to the coastline. When they had been going for some time, the boy grew so curious that he decided to open one eye just a little bit, even though he had been told not to. He opened his left eye ever so slightly.

And that was when he saw that Qillarsuaq had turned himself into a polar bear and was running in front of the dogs. Wherever the polar bear's paws touched the sea, it froze to ice so the dogs and sled could go over it.

Suddenly the ice began to crack, and one sled runner fell through, nearly throwing the boy off the sled. Then he understood that Qillarsuaq had been serious when he had warned the boy not to open his eyes, so the boy quickly pressed them shut again. The sled straightened up.

Eventually they stopped. Qillarsuaq said:

"Right, you can open your eyes now."

The boy did so and realized they were back onshore. Qillarsuaq had his usual human shape again and was standing next to the sled.

"Now take a look back," he said.

The boy looked over his shoulder. The ice he had seen when he opened his eyes had disappeared, and only the frothing waves remained!

So if he hadn't known it already, the boy now had proof that Qillarsuaq was a great shaman.

THE DOG WITH THE TOP KNOT

Once upon a time, there were two big girls. They were very shy, so whenever they needed to pee they wouldn't sit on the pot in the house like everyone else, but would walk up to the mountains where no one could see them and squat up there.

One day one of them needed to pee. She asked the other girl to come with her, and together they walked some distance away from the house.

They both pulled their trousers down and squatted. Suddenly they saw a dog. It was a very unusual dog—it had a top knot between its ears.

"Help," said one of the girls. "A dog with a top knot. This is very strange. Something is definitely not right."

They quickly finished their business and pulled up their trousers, but when they turned to go home, the dog blocked their path so they couldn't leave. It herded them farther inland, and they were too scared to do anything other than obey it.

Finally they reached a small house. It appeared to belong to the dog because it nudged them through the door.

Once they were inside the house, the dog lay down and blocked the exit.

The girls looked at one another. What were they going to do? Every time they tried to leave, the dog would growl at them.

They knew this was no ordinary dog. Dogs don't have top knots. Perhaps it was bewitched. Perhaps it was an evil spirit.

One of the girls had an idea.

"Do you happen to know a spell to make it fall asleep?" she said.

The other girl didn't. "Do you?" she asked.

The first girl thought hard. Come to think of it, she did know a spell, but she wasn't sure if it worked with dogs. They decided to give it a try.

The girl said the spell she knew, and slowly the dog's eyelids grew heavier and heavier until it was fast asleep.

"Let's get out of here," said one of the girls. But before they dared to go, they wanted to be sure the dog was definitely asleep.

They approached it carefully. They poked its side. It didn't react. Then they tried pulling its tail. Again, nothing happened. Then they tried shaking it. The dog seemed to smile a little, but it didn't wake up.

Finally the girls found the courage to escape. They stepped over the dog, but one of them accidentally trod on its ear. The girls froze and stood very still. Would the dog wake up? No—again, it just seemed to smile before it carried on sleeping.

Phew! They breathed a sigh of relief once they were outside. Then they start to run. They ran as fast as they could home to their settlement.

When they were nearly home, one of them glanced over her shoulder—and in the distance saw that the dog was chasing after them. It had woken up and realized they had fled.

As soon as they reached their settlement, they shouted at the top of their voices:

"Run! We're being chased by a dog with a top knot. Run!"

The people from their settlement quickly realized that something was wrong. A dog with a top knot. This was no ordinary dog. It might be an evil spirit. So they pulled down their tents, gathered up everything they owned, and threw it all into big umiat. Then they climbed into the boats—the girls just managed to get on board—and rowed away from the coast as fast as they could.

When they were out on the water, they saw the dog go panting into the settlement. It ran down to the shore and barked at the boats, but luckily it didn't swim out into the water where they were.

Instead it started searching the settlement for things the people had dropped or not managed to pack in the rush.

It found a pair of short women's trousers and put them on. Then it found a plaited hairband and tied it around its top knot. Every time it found an item of women's clothing, it would put it on. At the end it looked almost like a woman.

It walked down to the shore again and looked at the boats that were sailing away. Then it turned around and slowly left the settlement. It walked back to its little house where the girls had been trapped.

When the people in the boats saw it go away, they were hugely relieved, but none of them ever dared go back to the settlement for fear that the dog might return.

KAMIKINNAQ AND THE GIANTS

In Noorsiit near Kulusuk lived a tiny boy who grew very slowly. His name was Kamikinnaq. Even when he was fully grown, he was no taller than a child.

He got a small qajaq, but both he and the qajaq were far too small to go seal hunting, so he could only catch black guillemot chicks.

He caught the black guillemot chicks by a lake just outside of Noorsiit, which was as far as he could paddle.

His parents didn't accept that he was so small because they said to him:

"What a wimp you are. Why don't you ever go seal hunting? After all, you have a qajaq."

This made Kamikinnaq angry, and he decided to leave his parents and the settlement.

As he left, he paddled right past the island where he usually caught black guillemot chicks and onwards out to sea. The hunters who were sitting in their qajait waiting for prey close to the shore said to one another:

"I wonder who that can be. It looks like Kamikinnaq, but he doesn't usually come as far as this. He must be mad to paddle out this far in such a small qajaq."

Kamikinnaq ignored them and continued paddling until he reached the next furthest qajait waiting for seals. Again the hunters wondered what Kamikinnaq was doing so far offshore in his small qajaq. They also thought he had gone mad.

But Kamikinnaq didn't even look at them. He finally reached the last qajait, which he

Black Guillemot

also passed—to the huge astonishment of the hunters. He paddled far out into the big, open sea, and the men in their qajait watched him disappear in the distance.

"He must be mad," they said. "He must have lost his mind. Paddling that far out in a small qajaq could kill you."

When they returned home to the settlement, they told the people what had happened. No one ever expected to see Kamikinnaq again.

Kamikinnaq continued to paddle farther out to sea until he saw a big iceberg. Or rather, he thought it was an iceberg, but when he came closer, he could see that it was a giant seagull that had come from the land on the other side, Akilineq, the country which today we call Canada.

Kamikinnaq didn't dare sail past the gull because he was afraid it might eat him, given how big it was. He paddled around it in a big arc and onwards until he spotted a big island.

When he came closer, he could see that what he thought had been an island was really a giant paddling his qajaq.

Kamikinnaq pulled up alongside the giant's qajaq and called out to him, but the giant was so tall that all he could hear was a tiny squeak. When Kamikinnaq kept shouting, the giant shook his head and said to himself, *What's that strange noise I keep hearing?*

Then he spotted the tiny qajaq farther down. He picked up Kamikinnaq in his glove and tucked him under the cross straps of his own qajaq. Then he began paddling home. He was so fast that Kamikinnaq's hair was flattened. When they approached the shore, Kamikinnaq saw a tall mountain that turned out to be the giant's house.

The giant called out to his wife when they reached the shore and a giant woman came out of the house.

"I have a surprise for you," the giant said. "We've always wanted a child, and now I bring you a foster child."

"Where is it?" the woman said, looking about.

"Here," the giant said, untangling Kamikinnaq from the straps. He passed him to his wife, who put Kamikinnaq in the palm of her hand and carried him up to the house.

She put him on a shelf in his qajaq, and there he sat for three days.

There is a saying that when you have caught something unusual, no one must touch it for three days.

When three days had passed, they took him down from the shelf and put him on the floor. There he sat for another three days.

One night Kamikinnaq discovered a giant monster coming towards him. He screamed and shouted as loud as he could, but no one heard his tiny human voice. He managed to get out of the qajaq and ran to the bench where his foster father was sleeping. But the bench was so high that it was impossible for him to climb it. Fortunately one of his foster father's long hairs fell over the side, and Kamikinnaq used it to climb up while he continued to shout:

"Help, help! A dangerous monster is after me. Help!"

It proved to be almost impossible for him to wake his foster father, but when he finally succeeded, the giant said in surprise:

"But where's the monster?"

"There," Kamikinnaq shouted. "Can't you see the huge monster over there?"

The giant laughed out loud.

"Do you mean that little flea?"

"Yes," Kamikinnaq shrieked. "It's a dangerous monster."

"Oh, that," the giant said, blowing the flea away. "You had better come up here with us."

And he put Kamikinnaq on the bench, where he fell asleep immediately.

Later Kamikinnaq woke up in the middle of the night with a jolt. He had heard a sound, and found another monster facing him.

He shrieked and managed after much difficulty to wake his foster father.

"Help, another monster," Kamikinnaq screamed, but the giant merely laughed at him.

"It's just a spider. It won't hurt you."

Then he blew on it and it, too, disappeared.

One day Kamikinnaq's foster father made a wooden bridge from the main bench to the bench by the window. Kamikinnaq was far too small to walk in and out of the house because he couldn't climb up or down the main bench, so now he got the chance to look out of the window instead.

His foster father pointed out of the window to two mountains separated by a deep gorge.

"If one day you see that gorge fill up with a big, white animal, then I want you to shout as loud as you can: 'Bear, bear!'"

Every day Kamikinnaq would go to the window and look outside, and one day he did indeed see a big, white animal emerge between the mountains.

"Bear, bear!" Kamikinnaq screamed.

His foster father rushed over and asked:

"Where do you see it?"

"There," Kamikinnaq screamed.

"That one? But that's just a fox," his foster father laughed. "But if you get dressed, then you can come hunting with me and we'll catch it."

He put Kamikinnaq in a fold in his *kamik* and went fox hunting. It didn't take him long to catch the fox and skin it.

As a reward for having spotted the fox, he gave Kamikinnaq a small piece of fox fat. But although it was only a tiny piece for the giant, it was so heavy for Kamikinnaq that he could barely drag it home.

When they came home, his foster mother was happy and proud that her foster child had helped catch a fox and been given his share of the prey, so she celebrated with freshly picked crowberries.

Another day as Kamikinnaq was walking back and forth at the window, he discovered that the gorge between the two mountains was completely full of something white—and that the whiteness was moving.

"Bear, bear!" he shouted.

His foster father looked out of the window and said:

"Yes, this time it really is a bear, but it's not a very big one."

They got ready to go hunting, and again the giant put Kamikinnaq into a fold of one of his boots, under the laces, so he wouldn't fall out in the heat of the hunt.

They went after the bear, they caught it, and they killed it. When the giant had skinned it, Kamikinnaq was given a tiny piece of blubber. It was no bigger than the small, hard lumps that are found inside blubber, but even that was so big he had to cut it in half to be able to drag it home on his back.

Yet again his foster mother was happy and proud of her little foster son.

One winter's day his foster father took Kamikinnaq salmon fishing. They reached a lake so big that Kamikinnaq couldn't see the shore on the other side. The lake was frozen over, and in the middle of the ice another giant was salmon fishing. A big pile of salmon lay on the ice next to him.

His foster father made a hideout for Kamikinnaq near the shore and said to him:

"Do you see that man fishing over there with only two teeth in his mouth? He's very embarrassed about that. I want you to shout as loud as you can: 'Boo-hoo, you only have two teeth, boo-hoo, you only have two teeth!'"

Kamikinnaq wasn't very keen to do that. He was scared the other giant might spot him and come after him.

"There's nothing to be afraid of," his foster father assured him. "If he comes after you, I'll deal with him. I'm much stronger than him."

Then Kamikinnaq wasn't afraid to do as his foster father told him. He shouted at the top of his lungs:

"Boo-hoo, you only have two teeth! Boo-hoo, you only have two teeth!"

When the salmon fisherman heard those words, he looked about to see where the noise was coming from. When he spotted Kamikinnaq's foster father, he grew furious and ran towards him to fight him. But the foster father was much stronger. He flung the fisherman against the ice and killed him, then took all the salmon he had caught.

As time went by, Kamikinnaq realised he had started to grow.

He grew and he grew, and he was soon as big as his foster father.

One day his foster father asked him whether he had family elsewhere.

Then Kamikinnaq told him that his parents lived at Noorsiit.

"Don't you want to visit them?" his foster father asked.

Kamikinnaq realized that his anger towards his parents had disappeared because he had grown and found a new place to live, so he decided to visit them again.

He got into the big qajaq he now had and paddled and paddled. When he reached his old settlement, he was so big that he could effortlessly put his hand on top of the big headland.

The people got very scared when they saw the giant in the big qajaq.

They couldn't recognize Kamikinnaq, so asked who he was.

"I'm Kamikinnaq, the boy you used to call a little wimp."

Then he went ashore and up to his parents' tent. He had grown so tall that he didn't fit inside the tent, and if he wanted to talk to his parents, he had to scoop them up in the palm of his hand.

Afterwards he went hunting to get plenty of food for his parents, who had grown very old while he had been away.

He paddled far out into the open sea and caught many harp seals, which he put in his qajaq. If they wiggled too much, he would grab them by the back flippers and bash their heads against each other, killing them.

It wasn't until he had caught enough seals so that his parents would have food for many, many years that he got ready to travel back to Akilineq.

He asked his parents and everyone else at the settlement to move their tents up to the highest mountain. He was afraid the waves and whirlpools his paddles would create when he started paddling home would flood the settlement. He helped his parents move their tent and the big pile of seals up the mountain. Some old people from the settlement moved their tents up there as well. Everyone else left their tents where they were.

When Kamikinnaq got into his big qajaq and started paddling away from the shore, enormous waves washed over the settlement. The waves were so high they almost reached the top of the mountain where his parents were sitting.

Everyone who hadn't moved their tents to the top of the mountain drowned in the ensuing flood.

Kamikinnaq paddled across the wide open sea, and his parents never saw him again.

Harp Seal

71

AQISSIAQ, WHO COULD RUN AS FAST AS A PTARMIGAN

Once upon a time, there was a man and his wife who had septuplets. All seven children were boys, and right from when they were very young, their father would teach them to run and undergo strength training so they would turn into strong men.

Some years later, the wife got pregnant again, but this time she gave birth to only one child. It was another boy, and they named him Aqissiaq, which means "ptarmigan chick."

No one really took an interest in Aqissiaq. The father was busy training his seven big brothers, so Aqissiaq was left alone much of the time.

Realizing that his father wouldn't be spending any time with him, Aqissiaq decided to train his strength on his own and teach himself to run very fast.

Eventually, he became so quick that he could run as fast as a ptarmigan. He became such a good ptarmigan hunter that he could catch six birds with only a small stick as his weapon.

When he saw a brace of ptarmigan, he would kill one of them with his stick, and when the others tried to fly away, he would run underneath them and grab their legs. He only ever caught six at once simply because that was the number he could hold in his hands at any one time—otherwise he would have caught more.

One year the winter was very harsh, and all the animals disappeared. You couldn't even catch ptarmigan. Yet Aqissiaq would still go out every day to see if there was something edible to catch.

One day he had wandered off in a direction he didn't usually go. There had not been anything he could hunt, but on his way home he spotted something big and black that hadn't been there on his way out. He carefully approached it to see what it was and discovered it was a giant worm.

He crept up on the worm, took out his knife, and plunged it into the side of the animal. The worm turned to the side where it had been hurt, but Aqissiaq was already on the other side, where he also stabbed it. He continued like that, moving so quickly that he was always on the opposite side that the worm expected.

The blood was spurting out in jets from where Aqissiaq had stabbed it, and when he thought it had had enough, he ran home as fast as he could. But although Aqissiaq was a fast runner who could catch flying ptarmigan, the worm was still faster than him and soon caught up. Then the battle continued the same way, with Aqissiaq always where the worm thought he wasn't.

Finally the worm had been stabbed so many times and had lost so much blood that it started to feel weak. Aqissiaq decided to run home again when he, too, started to feel weak. It was as if he had lost all his strength. He fainted and collapsed.

When he woke up, he could see that the worm was lying dead a short distance away from him. He wondered whether it was edible. When people are starving, any kind of meat is valuable.

He cut open its side and found plenty of fat under its skin. He tasted it. It actually tasted very nice, so he cut out as big a chunk of meat as he could carry and went home.

When he returned to his settlement, he told everyone what he had experienced and gave them some of the meat he had brought back. Everyone was hungry and wanted more, so many people decided to make their way to the worm, although it was the middle of the night.

Aqissiaq told his family it was better to wait until the next morning, when they would walk up there together.

At daybreak they headed out, but when they had been walking for some time, they came across a dead man, and soon afterwards another one—all the way up to the worm lay dead men. Some were clutching big pieces of meat, but they had collapsed because they hadn't been strong enough to carry such heavy things. Others had been so weakened and emaciated by hunger that they hadn't even reached the worm.

Aqissiaq and his seven strong brothers cut off as much meat as they could carry and brought it home. Later they went back for more, but the worm was so big that they hadn't managed to eat it all by the time winter was over.

The next two winters were also very harsh, and again all the animals left. Aqissiaq still went out every morning to catch ptarmigan, although he was rarely successful. One day when he was at the top of a mountain, he saw what looked like a foggy bank far across the frozen sea. He wondered whether it might be a hole in the ice, and if so, maybe animals had gathered near the open stretch of water.

He told his father that he would go to the hole in the ice the following day to see if there was anything to catch. He told his family not to worry if it was a long time before he came home.

It had barely grown light the next morning before he set out. He ran across the ice and didn't reach the hole until noon. He was delighted because it turned out that the hole in the ice was full of eider ducks.

He started catching them with snares. He caught many and could have stayed for longer but had to stop in order to get back before it grew dark again. Before he began walking, he counted that he had caught sixty birds.

When he came home, he told his family about the many eider ducks that were trapped in the hole in the ice and suggested that his brothers come with him the next day.

They left at sunrise and made their way to the hole in the ice. Some of the brothers caught white males, and others caught black females. Aqissiaq caught only black females. They caught birds all day long, but when it was time to go home, the sky clouded over—a storm was brewing. Soon they were battling a violent southwesterly storm, and just when they were nearly home, they saw that the ice was starting to break up and drift away from the shore. Aqissiaq said to his brothers that if they jumped ashore first, then he would throw the birds to them. So that was what they did, and finally Aqissiaq himself jumped ashore.

They had plenty of food all winter, and when spring came and the ice finally melted, they still had birds left.

Aqissiaq's father had once told him about a man who lived near Ilulissat. He was said to be so strong and so fast a runner that he was stronger and faster than anyone else.

Aqissiaq, who by now had grown into a big and strong young man, couldn't forget his father's story, so one day he decided to find this man and ask him if he wanted to race.

"Don't worry about me," he said to his father and his brothers. "I'll be fine."

And off he went to Ilulissat.

When Aqissiaq found the man, he was busy ice fishing outside his settlement. He had built an *iglu* and was standing up inside it, fishing. Every time he caught a halibut, he would throw it outside. When he looked out of the iglu, he could see a tiny black dot in the distance. It was so small to begin with that he thought it was a raven. But the dot soon grew bigger, and he decided that it might be a fox. Then he went back inside his iglu.

After he caught another halibut, he took it outside. This time he could see that it was a human being approaching. He couldn't understand it, because he had only been inside a brief moment and now the man was very close to him—he must have run very fast. The stranger was tall and appeared to be a good runner.

Aqissiaq stopped and caught his breath as he bashed his stick so hard against the ice that ice splinters flew up around him.

Then he said, almost to himself:

"I've heard that a very strong man, who is a great runner, lives around here. I would like to race him."

"I'm that man," the man said.

"Then let's race one another," Aqissiaq said.

The man was happy to do so, and they started running towards the shore as fast as they could. But it appeared that they were equally fast.

The man's wife was standing on the shore emptying a chamber pot when she saw her husband come running with a stranger.

I wonder who that can be, she thought.

When they came very close to the thick border of ice floes down by the shore, they disappeared out of sight, but soon reappeared and took off in a great leap, landing on the smooth ice, where they glided along next to each other. One wasn't in front, and the other wasn't behind.

Once they had raced one another and could see that they were equally fast, they went back to the iglu and caught more halibut.

That evening when they returned to the settlement, the man said to his wife:

"We've been visited by someone who might not be a real human being. He's so big that we'll have to open up the entrance tunnel for him to get inside the house."

And so they did, in order for Aqissiaq to get inside. There wasn't much room for him inside, either. He was too big to sit on the bench, and they had to put some furs on the floor for him to sit on.

The wife cooked for them, and both she and her husband showed great hospitality towards Aqissiaq.

After they had eaten, Aqissiaq suggested a test of strength. The man was happy to oblige and joined Aqissiaq on the floor. The men sat facing one another with their legs entangled. Then they started pulling each other's arms. They wanted to see who could first straighten out the other man's bent arm.

Aqissiaq was left-handed, so his left arm was his stronger. The man was right-handed, so his right arm was his stronger. They started with the left arm, and it didn't take long before Aqissiaq straightened out the man's arm so violently that with one pull he tore the skin off his wrist. Then they tried again, this time using the right arm. This time it was Aqissiaq who quickly had his arm straightened out so violently that he, too, had all the skin ripped off. In that respect, they were also equal.

The next morning Aqissiaq decided to go home. The man followed him on his way, and when they reached the iglu where they had first met, Aqissiaq said:

"Now I'm going to run home with the same speed I usually keep when I'm out walking."

Both men were happy to have gotten to know one another and to have met an equal.

"Now that we know one another, you must promise to visit me every now and then."

Aqissiaq promised to do that, and then he started to run homeward. He ran so quickly that the snow flew out behind him like a cloud, and the sunlight was broken by snow crystals, creating a rainbow.

The man watched him until he could see him no longer.

THE GIRL WHO WOULDN'T SLEEP

In the old days, people said that children should go to bed early—much earlier than adults.

If children refused to go to sleep, people would say to them:

"If you don't go to bed, then Iikkaleq will come get you."

This really scared the children.

Iikkaleq was a woman with giant nostrils. Her nostrils were so big they reached right up to her eyes. And the children were scared of her.

If the children still refused to go to sleep after the adults had threatened them with Iikkaleq, they would be told the story of Qattaatsiaq.

Qattaatsiaq was a little girl who would never climb onto her bench to sleep at night. When she was told to go to bed, she refused. She would rather keep playing. Even when she was so tired that she nearly keeled over and would yawn again and again, she still refused to go to sleep. Not even when the adults warned her that if she yawned as much as that, then she would end up looking like Iikkaleq.

One evening she was sitting on the floor playing with her dolls as usual. Everyone else in the house had long since gone to bed and was fast asleep.

Suddenly she heard someone puttering about in the entrance tunnel to the house, and moments later a woman appeared in front of her. She looked absolutely dreadful—and her nostrils were so big that they reached all the way up to her eyes.

The woman said to Qattaatsiaq:

"Come with me and bring your dolls."

Qattaatsiaq didn't dare do anything other than obey, yet she tried to talk her way out of it:

"I don't have any kamiik to wear," she said.

"Then put on your mother's."

"But I haven't got an *annuraaq*," Qattaatsiaq tried again.

"Then put on your mother's."

So Qattaatsiaq had no choice other than to put on her mother's kamiik and annuraaq coat and follow the woman.

Outside it was a dark night, and Qattaatsiaq wondered where they were going.

The woman took her to the dunghill where people from the settlement dumped all their rubbish. She showed Qattaatsiaq an entrance that the girl had never noticed before.

They entered a room where everybody looked just like Iikkaleq—they all had giant nostrils.

Qattaatsiaq wanted to run away, but she was too scared to move.

Suddenly she heard a splash. The people who lived in the house above had emptied a big bucket of pee onto the dunghill, and it ran right into the room of those below.

People ducked and tried to pinch their giant nostrils to avoid the smell. Qattaatsiaq had to pinch her nose as well because the smell was so bad. *Yuck!*

Shortly afterwards she heard another splash. *Oh no, there's more,* she thought. And there was. However, this time it wasn't pee, but lovely meat soup. The people above had tipped a whole pot of soup onto the dung heap.

Everyone threw themselves at the soup and gobbled it down. They were very happy because they had no food of their own.

But when pee was tipped out again they would curse their upstairs neighbours.

When Qattaatsiaq's family woke up the next morning, they couldn't understand where Qattaatsiaq could be. And her mother's kamiik and annuraaq were also gone. How mysterious.

They searched high and low, and asked everyone from the settlement if they had seen the little girl, but gone she was, and gone she stayed.

Finally, her parents stopped looking for her—they thought they would probably never see their little girl again. They were very sad.

A whole year passed, but her parents never completely abandoned hope that one day Qattaatsiaq would return.

One evening they suddenly heard someone in the entrance tunnel to their house.

"Who is it?" they called out.

"It's me, Qattaatsiaq."

At first her parents were delighted, but when they saw their daughter, they were horrified. They could barely recognize her.

During the year she had been missing, she hadn't slept at all. She had been yawning and yawning—and had ended up looking like Iikkaleq with the giant nostrils.

Adults tell this story of Qattaatsiaq to their children when they refuse to go to sleep.

"If you don't go to sleep now, then Iikkaleq will come for you," they say to the children, and you can be sure that the children hurry off to bed and shut their eyes tightly, because no one wants to live for a whole year under a dunghill like Qattaatsiaq and end up looking like Iikkaleq with the giant nostrils.

THE MOTHER OF THE SEA *OR* THE TWO LITTLE ORPHANS WHO SAVED THEIR SETTLEMENT

The town of Narsaq was once a big settlement with many people. The settlement was known for its two very skilled shamans.

It was also the home of two little orphans, a girl and her younger brother. Seeing as they had no one to care for them, the people in the house where they lived made the children sleep in the coldest place: on a bench right below the window.

One year the winter was very harsh. The ice on the sea was so thick that the hunters couldn't find a single hole to catch seals or fish. Therefore there was great suffering at the settlement. People were starving, and since there was no one to look out for the two orphans, they got hardly any food. However, every now and again one of the hunters would feel sorry for them and give them a little of his own food.

One morning the hunters went out as usual to see if the weather had improved or if there were any holes in the ice where they could catch something for the people from the settlement to eat. But everything was frozen over. There wasn't even a tiny patch of clear water in sight.

They went to their great shamans and said:

"If the frost and the cold carry on, we'll all starve to death. You must summon the spirits so they can get us some animals."

The shamans were happy to help, and that evening they invited people from the other houses over to watch their ritual. Many people came, and the house was soon filled to the rafters.

The lamps were extinguished, and once it was pitch black, the two shamans began. The people heard one of them go into the entrance tunnel to the house, while the other sat in the far corner of the main bench.

Everyone waited with bated breath for the shamans to say something—but not a sound came from either of them. The people waited and waited and began to grow very impatient.

Suddenly they heard the little orphan girl say from her bench by the window:

"The two great shamans aren't saying anything. I don't think they're shamans at all. Let's light the lamps again."

And so they did. The two shamans got up, red-faced, and lay down on the bench with their heads dangling over the edge. They didn't say anything when people spoke to them, they were so embarrassed.

The house was full of people who had been looking forward to the ritual, and many were annoyed that the lamps had been lit again, so they turned on the little girl and yelled at her. Even the hunter, who was usually nice to the two orphans, grabbed the girl, hit her, and shouted:

"What do you know about shamanism? You just keep your mouth shut and wait for the great shamans to say something."

He had hit the girl hard, and she cried and cried, but when she had calmed down, she crawled up onto the window bench and said:

"I would like a skin big enough to make a whole qajaq, a skin no one has cut anything from."

One of the hunters went to get it. When he returned with it, the little girl said:

"Put it on the floor and smooth it out so no part of it is crumpled up."

The people did so, and when the skin was very smooth, the girl climbed down from the bench, and her little brother followed.

She stood on the skin and started spinning around. Her younger brother did the same. They twirled and they twirled, and slowly they started drilling their way through the skin with their big toes. People looked at them with amazement and curiosity as the children drilled deeper and deeper through the floor. The people didn't believe their own eyes when finally all they could see of the girl was her top knot. Very soon it, too, disappeared. Then her younger brother followed suit: he spun around—right down through the floor—and then he disappeared as well.

The people rushed over to the window to see if the children would emerge from the ground somewhere else. And quite right. Soon they saw a top knot appear just below the dunghill, spinning around and around, and soon the rest of the girl's body emerged. Her brother followed behind her, also spinning. Like spinning tops they whirled down towards the sea, through the ice growlers that sloshed about at the water's edge.

In this way the two siblings continued to spin down to the bottom of the sea. From there they travelled far towards the north. They reached a very strong eddy. On its surface three small pieces of ice were whirling around. Sometimes they were together, and at other times scattered apart. The children didn't know how to cross the eddy, but when three growlers came together for a moment, the big sister jumped up and used them as stepping stones to reach the other side of the eddy. Her brother followed, and he, too, reached the other side, safe and sound.

The big eddy was the belly button of the sea.

They carried on their journey towards the north. Eventually they saw a big house. They walked right up to it. It was amazing. Wonderful!

The cooking stations in the entrance tunnel to the house were practically plastered with whole seals waiting to be skinned, leaning up against the wall, and outside the house lay big piles of narwhals also waiting to be skinned.

The two siblings who had starved for such a long time were overwhelmed by this abundance of food.

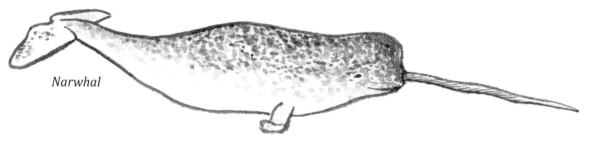

Narwhal

They wanted to enter the house but heard the sound of a big river cascading through the entrance tunnel. They were very discouraged because it was the only way to access the house. But then they discovered there was a path as narrow and sharp as the edge of a knife across the river.

They walked carefully up onto it and balanced on it across the wild, foaming river until they reached the house itself.

Here they heard groaning and complaining, someone shouting out loud and raging. When they entered, they saw a big woman sitting with her back to them, wailing and screaming.

They walked up to her and could see that her hair wasn't in a top knot as women's hair usually is, but that it was loose and matted with dirt and rubbish. When they looked more closely, they realized that her nose, eyes, and ears were filled with rags.

They had found the Mother of the Sea. She who rules the animals of the sea.

The old people tell us that all the rubbish and dirt people throw into the sea sticks to the Mother of the Sea. Their thoughtless behaviour makes the Mother of the Sea so angry that she withholds all the animals as punishment, and that causes starvation and suffering around the settlements.

As you can imagine, the children quickly got to work. The sister washed and brushed the woman's hair, and the brother picked the rags out of her nose, eyes, and ears.

When the woman was finally clean and free of all the dirt that had stuck to her, she made herself comfortable on her bench. She sat there for quite a while without saying anything. Then she moved a lamp, and a small creature leapt out from underneath it and practically flew towards the exit. The girl jumped up and snatched a few hairs from its back, and just as it reached the entrance tunnel to the house, she could see its back flippers. It was a small common seal.

Soon afterwards another animal appeared. Again, the girl jumped up and pulled a few hairs out of its back. It was a spotted seal.

And then all sorts of animals poured out—seals, walruses, and finally, a whale. All the animals were released back into the sea.

Then the Mother of the Sea said:

"Now I've freed all the animals, but when you get back home, I want you to tell the hunters from your settlement to catch only one seal a day for the first five days. Afterwards they can catch as many as they like."

The children said goodbye, but they were terrified of the dangerous

river in the entrance tunnel with the knife's-edge path. How would they cross it again?

However, when they reached the entrance tunnel, the river had disappeared, and instead there was lovely, soft, white sand they could walk on. All the frozen seals that had been lined up in the entrance tunnel and the narwhals outside were also gone.

The children set out on their journey home and travelled south for a long time on the bottom of the sea. Meanwhile they talked about the dangerous eddy that they would have to cross at some point. They were scared they wouldn't be able to jump onto the three small growlers that had first taken them across the eddy. They travelled for a long time, and suddenly, without having seen anything of the eddy, they found themselves back at the shore by the settlement where they had first drilled into the ground.

The house where they lived was still full of people. They had kept a lookout through the window to see if the children would return. But it had been two days since the children had disappeared, so by now most people had given up hope they would come back alive.

Suddenly someone called out:

"Look! Look at the shore."

Everyone ran to the window, and now they could see a top knot emerge from between the growlers at the water's edge. It spun and it spun, and the rest of the girl appeared, soon followed by her brother. And they whirled their way up to the front of the house, where they drilled themselves into the ground again.

Everyone in the house sat down and stared at the floor with great anticipation. No one said a word. And look, there they came—up through the qajaq skin, which was still lying outstretched on the floor. First the little orphan girl and then her brother. Spinning and spinning.

The two children sat down on the bench below the window. Everyone looked quizzically at the girl. Then she told them what the Mother of the Sea had said to them. And she pleaded with all the hunters to catch only one seal a day for the next five days.

After she had told them the story of their journey, everyone decided to go home. But when they went outside, the sea was still covered by ice and there was no opening to be seen, something that made many people doubt that what the little girl had said could really be true.

But that night there was a violent storm. The wind was howling and squealing. And when the people came out of their houses the next morning, they saw that the ice had broken up, and there was a big stretch of open water right in front of them. In the far horizon they could see big pods of narwhal.

It was very tempting for the hunters to catch as many as they could, given how many animals were right in front of them, but everyone obeyed the Mother of the Sea. No one caught more than one seal.

Now people had meat and could fill their bellies for the first time in a long time. And this time they didn't forget the two little orphans. They asked them to join in and eat all the meat they could, but the children climbed down from the window bench and modestly took only a small piece of meat before they hurried back to their usual place by the window.

The next day the hunters went out again, and that evening they brought home one seal each. When one of the women was busy preparing the seal, she said:

"Oh, look. Someone has pulled hairs out of the fur on the back of this seal."

Then the little girl said:

"It was me who pulled out the hairs, because I wanted that skin for a new pair of trousers."

She was given the skin immediately.

A few days later one of the men caught a big spotted seal.

"How odd," he said. "There are hairs missing from its fur."

Again, the little girl said:

"Yes, I pulled out the hairs because I thought it was such a beautiful piece of skin. I would like it for a pair of trousers."

Seeing as the girl and her brother had saved the whole settlement from starving to death, they were also given that skin. The people were very grateful, and from then on the two little orphans were given all the food they could eat.

THE RAVEN THAT MARRIED A WILD GOOSE

Once upon a time, there was a big, black raven. He very much wanted to get married, but hadn't been able to find a wife. All the female ravens he had asked said no. One day he saw a little sparrow looking very sad.

The sparrow had just lost her husband and was crying and feeling very lonely. She had been married to her husband for many years, and he had always brought her the juiciest, fattest worms.

"Why are you crying?" the raven asked in a kind voice.

"I'm crying because I've lost my husband," the sparrow said. "We were together for such a long time, and he did everything he could to make me happy. He would always find me such lovely worms."

The raven thought this might be an opportunity to get himself a wife.

"You don't need to cry anymore," he said. "I'll marry you. Look how handsome I am. Look at my fine, black feathers, my large beak, and my high forehead. I'll find you worms, and at night you can snuggle up under my wings."

But the sparrow didn't fancy the raven, despite his fine, black feathers and the other things he boasted of. She missed her husband and wasn't interested in the big raven at all.

Now, the raven was very insulted by that, of course. He couldn't understand why no one found him handsome and attractive.

"Well, suit yourself," he said, and puffed up his feathers before flying on.

Everywhere he went, he looked for a wife. He was desperate to get married.

One day he saw a flock of wild geese about to head south. He selected a single female, puffed up his feathers, and said in an ingratiating voice:

"Some sad little sparrow turned me down, can you believe it? She doesn't know what she is missing. However, now I would like to marry you."

"Sorry, no," the goose said. "I'm about to fly south with my flock."

"No problem," the raven said. "I'll just come with you."

"That'll never work," the geese said in unison. "We have a long journey ahead of us, and whenever we need to rest, we do so on the sea. But you can't do that. Your feathers aren't waterproof like ours, and there are no icebergs along the way where you can sit."

"I'm great at flying," the raven boasted. "I can float for a very long time without using my wings—that's how I rest. Or I can fly back and forth across the sea while you're resting."

The wild goose couldn't think of any more objections, and so she married the raven.

The other geese didn't want the raven to come with them, but he insisted that he would. In the end they gave up and said:

"If you really think you can keep up, then come with us. Let it be on your own head. We won't help you when you collapse from exhaustion and drown."

Soon afterwards the geese took off. The raven followed as best he could, and to begin with, everything was fine. When the geese rested on the water, the raven would fly on ahead and turn back to join them when he reckoned the geese had finished resting.

However, after some time the raven began to lag behind. He wasn't used to flying so far for as long as the geese, and he grew dreadfully tired.

"Wait for me," the raven called out to his wife.

The wild goose wasn't keen to leave her flock to look after her raven husband, but even so, she landed on the water so he could rest on her back.

The raven was so exhausted that he fell asleep instantly, but his goose wife didn't want her flock to fly off without her. What if she couldn't find them again, or what if she couldn't catch up? So she nudged the sleeping raven into the water and flew after the other geese.

When the raven felt the icy water, he woke up with a start. In the distance he could see the flock of wild geese.

"Help!" he cried out fearfully in his hoarse raven voice. "Help! I can't swim or rest on the water. Please help me."

But neither the geese nor anyone else heard his cries. The raven drowned in the cold water, and his dead, black body sank to the bottom of the sea, where it slowly dissolved.

His soul turned into the black winged snails that live in the sea—the ones we call sea ravens.

ANNGANNGUUJUK, THE BOY WHO WAS ABDUCTED

Once upon a time, there was a small family of three—father, mother, and son—who lived alone in a settlement. The father was very strong and a good hunter.

One day the mother was cleaning the skin of a seal. The little boy, whose name was Anngannguujuk, was playing pretend qajaq in the entrance tunnel to the house. Every now and then his mother would call out to him, and he would reply.

But then the boy stopped replying when she called out. She called him several times, but there was still no reply. She went to look for him, but she couldn't see him anywhere.

She searched and she searched, but she still couldn't find him—not outside the house, by the shore, or up in the mountains behind the settlement. She was upset and also very scared of what her husband would say when he came home from hunting.

Soon she saw her husband's qajaq appear behind the last headland with a seal in tow.

When he had pulled the seal and his qajaq ashore, he asked: "Where's the boy?"

"I don't know. He disappeared shortly after you set out this morning. He was playing in the entrance tunnel, and suddenly he was gone. I've looked and looked, but I can't find him anywhere."

The man was furious with her for not taking better care of their little son, and he threatened to kill her.

"Please don't kill me," the mother pleaded. "Instead let us ask a shaman for help."

The husband agreed. He went off to find a shaman and came home with one shaman after the other. They summoned their helper spirits, but when they couldn't find the child, the father would chase them away without giving them anything to eat or drink.

Finally, he found a shaman who was known for being able to find

things that were missing. He invited the shaman home, and that night when it was dark, his guest got to work.

He summoned his helper spirits, and having spoken to them, he said to the parents:

"This isn't going to be very difficult. Your child is with the inland dwellers between two big mountains that face one another. An old couple live there, and they've taken him."

Inland dwellers were thought to have superpowers or be giants, so no sooner had the shaman spoken than he and the father headed up to the two big mountains. They walked for a long time until they finally spotted some houses. From one of the houses, smoke was coming from the air holes in the roof.

"It's heat that's pouring out," the shaman said. "Let's go over there."

They walked up and looked through the window. Inside they saw little Anngannguujuk sitting on the bench crying, while some of the inland dwellers walked around, and the two old people argued over whose turn it was to look after him.

"What do you want to eat?" they asked the child.

"Nothing," little Anngannguujuk sobbed.

"Do you want some caribou fat?"

"No."

When nothing could make him stop crying, they finally asked him:

"Do you miss your parents?"

"Yes," Anngannguujuk wailed.

The father grew very angry at this and wondered how to get his little son out of the house.

He said to the shaman:

"Can't you say a spell to make them fall asleep?"

The shaman started saying a spell, and one after the other the inland dwellers slumped onto the bench and started snoring. Eventually, only two were left awake. One of them started to yawn, and then fell asleep. The shaman had to use all his powers to make the last person fall asleep; finally, he started to yawn and fell asleep on the bench.

Anngannguujuk's father rushed inside the house and grabbed his son. But the child didn't have a stitch on him. All his clothes were hanging on the drying rack under the roof, and the house was so tall that first they had to find some long poles so they could get his clothes down.

Finally they left the house with the little boy and started their return journey. They walked all night, and it wasn't until the first rays of morning sunshine coloured the sky that they arrived home.

As soon as they were back at the settlement, they called out to the boy's mother. Then they cut the moorings of their umiaq, quickly threw all their possessions into it, and sailed out to some small islands.

No sooner had they set out to sea than they saw a big flock of inland dwellers come running towards the house.

When they discovered that the boy and his parents had fled, they were so angry that they smashed up the house, leaving nothing behind.

Ever since then, Anngannguujuk's parents never dared to settle on the mainland for fear of the inland dwellers, and instead they lived on the most distant islands.

And that's the end of the story.

TUNUTOORAJIK AND THE ONE-LEGGED GIANT

Once upon a time, there were two young men who were cousins. They lived in the same settlement, went qajaq hunting together—in fact, they did everything together. They weren't just cousins, but also the best of friends.

Once when they were out, they found a giant piece of driftwood. It was so big that they could make two *umiak* out of it. They agreed to see who could make the most beautiful boat, and to see who could finish first. So they decided to work away from each other and not meet until the boats were done.

Tunutoorajik had gotten off to a good start with his boat-building when an old man came up to him.

"Have you heard?" he said.

"Heard what?" Tunutoorajik said.

"Your cousin wants to kill you."

"I don't believe that," Tunutoorajik said. "He wouldn't dream of it."

When the old man realized that he couldn't make the two cousins fall out, he left.

Tunutoorajik ignored what the old man had said. He carried on making his boat as beautiful and as fast as he possibly could.

A little later the old man returned. Once again, he said:

"Your cousin wants to kill you."

"Never," Tunutoorajik said. "He would never do that."

But the old man got angry, and eventually Tunutoorajik started to believe him. So instead of finishing his boat and making it as beautiful as possible, he rushed the work and simply tried to finish it as quickly as possible.

The day before his boat would be ready, his cousin came over to him.

"Why are you doing such a shoddy job of making your boat? I thought we had agreed to make them as beautiful as we possibly could."

Tunutoorajik didn't know what to say to his cousin. He grew more afraid that the old man might be right after all and that his cousin really did want to kill him. All he said was:

"It takes such a long time. I haven't got the patience for it."

He looked deep into his cousin's eyes to see if there might be any hostility there, but he could see nothing but kindness. And yet he rushed to finish his boat. He didn't know what to think.

When he finished the skeleton for the boat, he lined it with skin the very same day.

And then he waited for his cousin to go hunting in his qajaq. As soon as he saw his cousin set off, Tunutoorajik quickly packed up his tent and threw it into the new umiaq. He told his wife to get into the boat, and they rowed away from the settlement as quickly as they could. His wife sat in the middle of the boat, rowing, and Tunutoorajik sat at the back, rowing and steering at the same time.

When his cousin returned that evening with his catch, his wife said to him:

"I don't understand why, but Tunutoorajik and his wife left today."

"But why, and where would they go?" the cousin asked.

"I don't know. They didn't say."

"Then I'll try to catch up with them and ask where they're going," the cousin said.

He quickly finished his umiaq and lined it with skin that very same day, and then he set off to find his cousin and good friend.

When he reached the first camp, he asked the people there if they had seen Tunutoorajik.

"Yes, he sailed past here yesterday," they said.

The cousin was so keen to get on that he didn't go ashore but rowed fast to catch up with Tunutoorajik. When he reached the next camp, he asked the people again.

"They sailed past the day before yesterday," the people said.

The cousin hurried on, and the next time he passed some tents, he asked:

"Have you seen Tunutoorajik?"

"Yes," they replied. "He sailed by three days ago."

Then the cousin stopped. He realized that he wouldn't be able to

catch up with Tunutoorajik and his wife, as they were getting farther ahead of him with every day. He turned the umiaq around, and as he made his way home, he wept at having lost his cousin. He was very fond of him, and they had been such good friends.

Tunutoorajik and his wife carried on rowing and hardly ever stopped. They fled to the south and didn't tell anyone where they were going.

Several days later, they reached an island in the sea. There was only a single house on the island, and so they went ashore. A big man came out of the house and walked down to meet them. Tunutoorajik could see that the man had only one leg.

The one-legged man asked them:

"Where are you going?"

"My cousin wants to kill me, so I've fled and am looking for some-where we can spend the winter."

"You're welcome to stay here," the one-legged man said. "I'm not scared of anyone."

The man was a giant, and his name was Ittuku.

When Tunutoorajik started to put up his tent, Ittuku said:

"You're welcome to stay in our house. There's plenty of room for you as well."

And that's how Tunutoorajik and his wife ended up living with the one-legged giant.

When they entered the house, they were very surprised to see many things made from iron, which the giant had hanging on his wall. There were knives and spears and even clothing made from iron. Now, get-ting hold of iron was difficult, so Tunutoorajik wondered greatly how the giant had managed to collect all those things.

One day the giant told him that whenever winter was coming, many ships would sail past the island through the narrow straits.

And quite right. After much time had passed and winter was com-ing, ships began to pass by. Every time a new ship came sailing through the sound, the giant would call out:

"Who are you?"

If they replied, "We're traders," the giant would let them pass.

If they didn't reply, he assumed they meant to harm him. Then he would put on one of the iron suits and limp down to the shore on his one leg with a giant whip. The whip was so long that it could reach across the sound. If the ship tried to pass, he would crack his whip so it wrapped itself around the mast, and the ship could sail no farther.

The crew onboard the ship would send a man up the mast with a knife to cut the whip. But the giant would just crack his whip again, and again it would wrap itself around the mast. Then he would pull the ship across to the island. All the sailors would jump ashore and flee, which made it easy for the giant to board the ship and take all the things he needed. He would usually empty the whole ship. This was how he had collected all those precious things made from iron.

Some time later, Tunutoorajik went outside the house. He discovered a big, white cloud that covered the whole of the western horizon, and it was approaching the island at great speed.

He went inside and said to the one-legged giant:

"I think we'll have a powerful southwesterly storm tonight."

The giant, however, didn't say anything, so everyone went to bed as usual.

The next morning when they woke up, they heard loud squawking and chirping outside the house.

Tunutoorajik wanted to get out, but he couldn't open the door. During the night, thousands of birds had landed around the house, and they had left a thick layer of bird poo everywhere. Tunutoorajik finally managed to force the door open, and it was a terrible sight everywhere he looked. Everything was covered in bird poo. He ran down to check on his umiaq, and it too was a sad sight. Only the tips of the front and back were sticking up. The rest of it was covered in poo, the weight of which was so heavy that it had snapped his umiaq in half.

Tunutoorajik rushed back inside and told the giant what had happened.

The giant took a spade and went outside. A little later, he came back in and said:

"Right, that's that sorted out."

When Tunutoorajik went back outside, he could see that the whole area in front of the house had been cleared and that his qajaq had been dug out and mended.

Tunutoorajik quickly got into his qajaq to go seabird hunting. When he had been paddling for some time, a big bird landed right on the front of his qajaq. It opened its beak and started talking like a human being:

"Look, I've settled right on the tip of your qajaq. Throw your bird spear and see if you can hit me."

Tunutoorajik threw his spear, but he missed the bird.

"Ha-ha, missed me," the bird said.

Another bird came swooping and settled right on the tip of his qajaq, just like the first bird.

"Try to hit me!"

Tunutoorajik threw his spear again, and this time he didn't miss. He carried on this way until he didn't have room to tie any more birds to his qajaq.

He was delighted to have caught so many birds, but when he brought his big catch home, the giant was furious.

Tunutoorajik didn't understand why and asked the giant's wife.

"I think it's because he usually talks to those birds," she said.

Tunutoorajik apologized profusely to the giant. He hadn't realized that the birds were special. The giant forgave him.

Tunutoorajik gave the birds to his wife, who cooked them and served them for dinner. The giant and his wife had never tasted boiled birds before, so they didn't know quite what to think, but when they had eaten a few, they couldn't stop because the birds were so tasty. They ate and they ate until they were full to bursting.

Then the giant said to Tunutoorajik:

"Feel free to go bird hunting any time you like. I hope you catch as many as you can tie to your qajaq."

And so Tunutoorajik went bird hunting every single day and brought home large quantities, until one day the birds left that part of the country, and that put an end to the delicious meals.

Winter had arrived, and it was very cold. One day Tunutoorajik came in and said:

"It's icy outside. The frost is severe."

"Was there a hollow in the snow when you peed?" the giant wanted to know.

"There was," Tunutoorajik said.

"Then it's not really cold yet," the giant said. "It's not properly cold until the stream of your pee freezes the moment it comes out of you."

A few days later Tunutoorajik went outside to pee—and quite right, his pee froze to ice immediately. He went back inside and told the giant about it. The giant said:

"That means the sea is freezing over. Go check if the ice can support you."

Tunutoorajik did so. There was ice everywhere as far as the eye could see. When he stamped his foot hard, the ice didn't even creak.

When Tunutoorajik woke up the next morning, the bench where the giant slept was empty. He had gotten up early to go hunting.

Tunutoorajik got ready to go hunting as well and followed him, but although he looked all day long, he never found the giant.

Soon after Tunutoorajik came home, the giant came back. He carried a big pile of meat on his back.

"Where did you get that from?" asked Tunutoorajik.

"I've been hunting bearded seals all day in the places where I usually find them," the giant said.

"I'll come with you tomorrow," Tunutoorajik said.

"That's not a good idea," the giant said. "Those places are so far away that only people who are very fast can get there."

Although the giant had only one leg, he was still much faster than Tunutoorajik, so Tunutoorajik decided not to go with him.

It was now the middle of winter, and it was dark all day and all night. The giant went outside to prop up his house with supports, and Tunutoorajik wondered why he did so.

The next morning, the people in the house were woken up by rumbling and growling outside. Tunutoorajik knew that the noises were those made by bears and quickly got dressed, but the giant stopped him and said:

"What you can hear outside are animals that can't be killed by ordinary human beings."

Then the giant took one of his long iron knives and went outside. It didn't take long before he came back in and said:

"Right, now there's work to do for ordinary human beings."

Tunutoorajik went outside with him and found dead bears everywhere. The men and their wives started skinning them, but there were so many that it took them a very long time to finish skinning the bears and cutting up all the meat.

After the bears had been to the island, the supports were taken off the house, but it wasn't long before the giant put them back in place. This time he did it even more carefully, and Tunutoorajik was very excited about what might turn up next.

One morning they heard sounds as if big, crawling animals were outside and on top of the house. The giant said:

"What we can hear outside this time is something which ordinary human beings can hunt."

Tunutoorajik quickly got dressed. He grabbed a long knife, and the giant took his whip.

The ground outside was completely covered with large walruses that were slithering around. Tunutoorajik and the giant started hunting them, and every time the giant hit them with his whip, they stretched out and died on the spot. The cold was so severe that they froze solid the moment they died. The animals' thick skin cracked in the frost as they died, and so Tunutoorajik could easily cut them up with his knife.

In that way the whole winter passed, and they never went hungry, not once. The big animals that came past the settlement provided them with plenty of meat and blubber.

Tunutoorajik's wife was going to have a baby, and when the baby was born, it had only one leg. They agreed that the giant must be the father of the baby, and all of them celebrated the birth with great joy.

Both families lived happily together and were always very lucky at hunting. Tunutoorajik and his wife spent the rest of their lives with the one-legged giant, and they never returned to their old settlement.

ALORUTTAQ THE ORPHAN

Not far from Kulusuk lived a hunter who had a foster child. The child's parents had died, so the foster father ought to be especially kind to the poor child. But he wasn't. He let the boy starve, and didn't give him proper clothes to wear or anything to put on his feet. And the boy had no toys at all.

The boy was called Aloruttaq, which means "the one who has nothing to put on his feet."

One winter the sea froze over, making it impossible to catch anything. The people in Kangaarsuk, which was the name of the settlement, were starving and suffering greatly. When they couldn't bear being hungry any longer, they made their way to another settlement called Siorartooq. There, people still had seals stored in their caches.

It was a long way to Siorartooq, and the people were weak from hunger. Aloruttaq followed them as best he could, but he had only flimsy rags to wear and nothing on his feet. The cold was biting because it was

Meat Cache

the middle of the winter. The boy was so cold that he shivered. With every step he took in the snow with his bare feet, he would stop and warm one foot with the other. This caused him to lag far behind, so when he finally got there, he was practically dead from cold.

The people of Siorartooq had taken out a whole seal for their starving guests, and there was still quite a lot of food left when Aloruttaq eventually arrived. But just as he was about to eat, his evil foster father stopped him:

"Now don't go eating all the food so there's nothing for the adults," he said, and Aloruttaq, who was very frightened of his foster father, was too scared to eat anything.

One day the people of Siorartooq brought pieces of meat to Kangaarsuk, and there was also a portion for Aloruttaq: two big ribs with plenty of meat on them. As Aloruttaq was about to sink his teeth into the meat, his wicked foster father took one rib from him and cut the meat off the other so that Aloruttaq had only a stripped piece of rib to gnaw on.

Another time, Aloruttaq's settlement was invited to Siorartooq to eat. Aloruttaq very much wanted to join in, but he nearly gave up on going. The trip would be very hard for him, and he had almost no strength left. However, if he stayed behind at the settlement, he wouldn't get any food at all, so he joined the others. Yet again he had to walk barefoot through the snow, and yet again he warmed one foot on top of the other after every step.

When he arrived, the others were busy eating a seal, which the people of Siorartooq had dug out of their cache. But yet again his foster father was after him and forbade him to eat anything.

The man whose house they were in overheard this and said to Aloruttaq's foster father:

"Please let the poor child eat as much as he can. He's in a sorry state. And there's plenty of food for all of us."

Despite what the man had said, Aloruttaq still didn't dare eat anything. He was so frightened of his wicked foster father.

The man noticed this and said to Aloruttaq:

"Oh, Aloruttaq, could you give me a hand with something out by the cache?"

Aloruttaq was happy to, but when the man saw his rags and bare feet, he said:

"You can't go out like that, without any warm clothing and bare-footed."

"I walked like this all the way from home, so I can easily come with you to the cache," Aloruttaq replied.

The man couldn't bear to see the poor boy go out in the cold and the snow with hardly any clothes, so he told his wife to give Aloruttaq some of his old clothes and kamiik he no longer used.

Once Aloruttaq was dressed, he began sweating profusely because he wasn't used to being so warmly dressed.

The people had carried a big hooded seal into the house for the starving people from Kangaarsuk, and when they had eaten all they could, the leftovers were put back in the cache. That was the job that the man wanted Aloruttaq to help him with.

When they were finished, Aloruttaq was given a shoulder with plenty of meat on it as a thank you.

"It's yours—and yours alone," the man said.

Aloruttaq couldn't believe his eyes when he got so much meat. He quickly hid it somewhere his foster father wouldn't find it.

When the people from Kangaarsuk were getting ready to go home, the man asked Aloruttaq:

"Would you like to stay here with us? My wife and I don't have any children, and I really like you."

Aloruttaq would have liked nothing more, but he didn't dare ask his wicked foster father for permission. He was afraid that his foster father would punish him and find new ways to torture him.

"Don't you worry about that," the man said. "I'm much stronger than your foster father, so if there are any problems, I can handle them."

So that was what happened.

Aloruttaq lived with the man and his wife. They took good care of him and gave him plenty to eat and warm clothing, and soon he began to grow and put on weight.

In time he became a very skilled hunter. He was very grateful to his new foster parents and helped them as much as he could. He was brave and had great stamina when he went hunting in his qajaq, and

soon he was the best hunter in the settlement. He provided food not just for his foster parents, but also for many others in the settlement. And he got himself a beautiful and lovely wife.

Some years later, there was a terribly severe winter. The sea froze over, and there wasn't a single hole in the ice where you could catch seals. Aloruttaq said to his foster father:

"If only I had some dogs, then I could go hunting across the ice with the sled."

"You're welcome to take my dogs," his foster father said. "They're just waiting around, and I'm not using them myself."

This made Aloruttaq very happy because his foster father had very strong and sturdy dogs. He attached them to the sled and set out across the ice.

He followed a large crack until he suddenly spotted a big, dark lump in the distance. When he came closer, he could see that it was a huge walrus with big tusks warming itself in the sunshine.

He stopped the dogs and wondered how to kill it. If he harpooned it and it slipped into the water, his hunting straps would not be able to pull out such a heavy weight.

As he sat wondering how to solve the problem, he discovered that an old male polar bear had also spotted the walrus. It crept up on the sleeping walrus while trying its best to hide between some big growlers that had stranded.

The walrus was soaking up the sun and had no idea that two different hunters were eyeing it. It slapped its big flippers to get rid of some lice that were bothering it, then grunted briefly before going back to sleep.

When the polar bear came closer and realized just how big the walrus was, it had second thoughts. It had to come up with a strategy to kill the big animal without risking its own life.

It found a big lump of very hard ice that it started gnawing at and shaping into a big ball. Then it held the ball with its front paws, very carefully approached the sleeping walrus, reared up on its hind legs, and hurled the lump of ice at the head of the walrus as hard as it could. It was such a powerful throw that the lump of ice turned into powdered snow. Then the polar bear started bashing the head of the walrus with its enormous paws.

The walrus was so stunned that, for a moment, it couldn't defend itself. When the bear sat down to rest, the walrus tried to get up to attack the bear, but it had no strength left, and blood was pouring out of its mouth. It twitched a bit, slammed its mighty back flippers into the ice, and then it died.

The bear caught its breath and was about to enjoy its giant meal. Only this time it was Aloruttaq's turn to attack. He released his dogs and signalled for them to attack the bear.

Barking wildly, they dashed across the ice and pounced on the huge animal, which was so busy with its kill that it hadn't noticed its enemy at all. It reared onto its hind legs while the furious dogs tried to bite it. At the same time, Aloruttaq threw his harpoon as hard as he could, and it plunged right into the heart of the bear.

The bear shoved a mouthful of snow into its mouth, roared loudly, and tumbled backwards into a snowdrift, where it died.

Aloruttaq was shaking all over from the excitement. He couldn't believe his luck. Two huge animals at once! He took out his knife and started the big job of skinning them. He thought about how happy people would be back at the settlement, where many were starving. He attached some big lumps of meat to the sled along with the bear-skin and left the rest behind. He attached the dogs to the sled once again and made his way home.

Back at the settlement, Aloruttaq's wife was waiting for him. She paced up and down, scanning the ice. She was a little worried because he had been gone a very long time. She hoped he was all right.

But then she spotted a tiny dot in the distance. It came closer and closer, and soon she could see that it was Aloruttaq's sled. It wasn't going as quickly now—perhaps it meant he was carrying a heavy catch.

"Have you caught a bear?" she called out to him when he was within earshot.

"Yes, and a giant walrus!"

It was almost too good to be true. All the people from the settlement came out of their houses and gathered around the sled. They were starving and skinny, so the prospect of meat for their cooking pots put a smile on everyone's face. They sent messages to the surrounding settlements, which were also suffering from starvation.

The next day, people from near and far came pouring in. The visitors included Aloruttaq's wicked foster father.

The men gathered all the dogs they could and drove out onto the ice to collect the remains of the bear and the walrus.

Once they got there, Aloruttaq cut up the remains of the animals and shared the meat among everyone who had turned up. He gave them big portions because he knew there was hunger and suffering in every settlement due to the harsh winter. He was covered in walrus blubber, and the animal's blood dripped from him as he went from man to man with a chunk of meat for each of them. When he reached the wicked foster father, he gave him just two walrus ribs with practically no meat on them.

The foster father asked why he got so little.

"It's payback for all the times when you gave me only a few ribs with no meat on them while everyone else ate until they were full."

The foster father was very embarrassed that everyone heard that. But then Aloruttaq went to his own pile of meat and took a big chunk, which he gave to his foster father after all. He thought he'd had his revenge.

After the meat had been distributed, everyone drove home happy with their share, but the wicked foster father was furious that Aloruttaq had humiliated him in front of the others. He wondered how best to take revenge, and decided to save the two walrus ribs that Aloruttaq had given to him. His plan was to make a *tupilak*—a kind of witchcraft figure— from them and get back at Aloruttaq that way.

When spring and summer came, the men were able to go hunting in their qajait again and provide food for their

Tupilak

families. The wicked foster father decided that the time had come to take his revenge on Aloruttaq.

He took out the two walrus ribs and carved a seal out of one of them—a seal with the magic power to kill Aloruttaq.

Every day Aloruttaq would go out in his qajaq and would always bring home several seals for his family and the others from the settlement. Until, one day, he caught nothing at all. It was as if the seals were avoiding him. He realized that somebody had bewitched the animals and wanted to harm him, perhaps even kill him.

He said to his wife:

"If one evening I don't return from hunting, I want you to go down to the shore where I normally pull up my qajaq. If you do that, you'll see all my hunting tools drift ashore one after the other. You'll discover that one item will be missing, and that will be my *kapussivik*—the cross straps on my qajaq. Don't be sad, I will come back to you. When I was born, a spell was put on me so that if I'm killed, I'll come back to life. The kapussivik will serve as a kind of qajaq for me on which I will sail around the earth. Because the world is so big, we who want to return to life must spend a whole year making this long trip. And so you must come back to the shore precisely one year after I am killed."

Although Aloruttaq told his wife not to worry, she worried all the same. She didn't want her husband to be killed, or to have to wait for him for a whole year.

Some days passed where Aloruttaq still caught nothing at all. Until one day a seal turned up right by his qajaq. He threw his harpoon and hit it. But the seal was behaving very strangely.

Aloruttaq started to suspect that the seal was bewitched. When it came closer to his qajaq, he could see that it was a red monster with the head of a dog. It tried to upend his qajaq by jumping over it and diving under it, wrapping the hunting strap around it, and eventually it managed to pull the qajaq under so that Aloruttaq drowned.

That evening Aloruttaq's wife went down to the shore to wait for him to return with the day's catch. But no qajaq appeared. Instead, a harpoon drifted ashore. The next day she walked down there again, and over time all his hunting tools appeared. Then she realized that he

had been killed. She waited and she waited, and exactly one year later, she returned to the shore. But there was no sign of Aloruttaq.

What had happened to him was that he had sailed around the world using the kapussivik as his qajaq, and when he finally got back to his own settlement, he wanted to sail ashore. But the red monster with the dog's head had lain in wait for him and blocked his path every time he tried to come ashore. In the end he had to give up returning to life.

His wife finally gave up waiting for him. When he disappeared, she had been expecting a child, and she gave birth to a little boy. She called the boy Aloruttaq, after his father.

Aloruttaq grew up and took after his father in many ways. He was a good and helpful person, always caring for the weak, and he became a great hunter like his father, always bringing home plenty of food for his family. He even married his mother, so he took after his father in that respect as well.

Sadly, there was another way he took after his father. The spell that Aloruttaq's wicked foster father had cast on Aloruttaq also affected Aloruttaq's son. One day when he was out hunting in his qajaq, a seal appeared and started to behave strangely. And just like with Aloruttaq, it turned out to be a red monster that tried to sink his qajaq. Again, the monster managed to drag the qajaq down, and the young Aloruttaq drowned.

But when Aloruttaq was born, a spell had also been put on him, as had happened with his father once upon a time. First, all his hunting tools drifted ashore, then he sailed around the world with a kapussivik as his qajaq, and finally he returned to the small bay that led to his settlement.

But where his father had failed, Aloruttaq succeeded—he managed to get around the monster so he could return to the shore and come back to life.

He rejoined his family, and everyone was delighted to see him again. Especially his wife—and mother—was happy because she had almost given up hope of ever seeing him again, as she'd had to do with his father.

However, their joy was sadly short-lived. When he entered the house, he was holding the kapussivik, which had served as his qajaq on his long trip around the world.

And when he put it down, someone in the house accidentally moved it so that it touched some blubber. Aloruttaq fainted immediately, because people who have returned from the dead can't tolerate something they had on their person touching blubber immediately after they have returned to life.

He was unconscious for a very long time, but when he woke up again, he was soon the same man he used to be, and he lived a good life with his family.

One day when he was out hunting, he came across the bewitched seal once more. This time he was prepared and flung his harpoon at it as hard as he could. It went right through the animal, and this time he managed to kill the monster before it could hurt him again.

And since that day, Aloruttaq's son, Aloruttaq, lived happily and well ever after.

THE WOMAN WHO MARRIED A DOG

Once upon a time, there was a couple who had a daughter. When she was old enough to get married, her mother suggested that she get herself a good husband.

There were plenty of men about, but the problem was that the girl didn't want any of them.

Eventually, her mother got so cross that her daughter didn't want a husband that she told their dog to marry her instead.

The dog did as it was told, and it lived in the house with the parents and the daughter.

As if the mother hadn't punished the daughter enough already by forcing her to marry the dog, she also ordered the father to take the girl to a small island. There she was to live on her own, because the dog wasn't allowed to come with her. There, she gave birth to a litter of puppies.

When the parents saw the dog trying to swim over to the island to be with its wife, they tied a big stone around its neck, and it drowned.

The father was in the habit of rowing across to the island with meat and food for the girl and the puppies.

The girl was furious with her parents for first forcing her to marry the dog and now isolating her on the island, so one day she said to the puppies:

"The next time your grandfather brings food, I want you to attack him and bite him to death."

And that's what the puppies did.

Then she placed them on the sole of a kamik and put them out to sea while she said:

"You'll end up living in such a way that you'll never want for anything."

It is said that the puppies drifted ashore in a distant country far away. There, they turned into white men—and it is believed that all white men are the descendants of these puppies.

THE GREAT FIRE *OR* HOW THE MUSSEL CAME TO BE

In the old days, a large group of people shared a big house near Simiutaq.

One evening all the grown-ups went off to a neighbouring settlement to take part in a song combat, and all the children were left at home, including a little orphan boy.

The children were having a great time and were making quite a racket in the house. The little boy kept trying to get the others to be quiet, but no one was listening to him.

The orphan boy really wanted to join in their game, but he couldn't bear the noise, and he was also scared of the dark, so he kept running in and out of the house as if he were frightened of something.

Once, after he had been outside, he came back in to tell the others that he had seen a big fire out at sea—and that it was heading for the shore.

The other children merely laughed at him. They didn't believe what he was saying.

He went back outside, and now he could see that the fire was much closer to the shore. Terrified, he ran back inside and told the others to watch out, but again, they just laughed at him and called him a wimp.

Then he asked them to lift him onto the drying rack under the roof. They didn't want to do that, but he kept pestering them. Finally they were so fed up with him that they lifted him onto the rack while they teased him and laughed at him.

He had only just gotten up there when a big, red glow that looked like the flare of a huge fire could be seen outside the house.

"What's that?" the children cried out, suddenly very scared. "What's that burning?"

The next moment a big fire swept through the entrance tunnel to the house. It had taken the shape of a monster and looked like a giant bearded seal that had been skinned.

The children panicked and ran around one another, but the monster used such a strong force that they were dragged towards it—and the moment they touched it, they dropped down dead.

The little orphan boy could see everything from his spot up under the roof. The power of the monster also beckoned him, but he clung to the drying rack and managed to escape its enormous power to attract things to it.

A little later, the monster and the fire withdrew. The boy climbed down and sat on his bench in despair. His dead friends were lying on the floor all around him.

And there he sat when the grown-ups returned from the neighbouring settlement. When they saw all the children on the floor, they laughed and said:

"Oh, it looks like you've had a lot of fun while we were gone. The children must have tired themselves out and collapsed."

When they realized that the children weren't asleep but dead, there was great despair and grief.

The little orphan boy told them what had happened, but none of the parents believed him.

"If what you say is true, then why aren't you dead as well? You killed them all."

"No, I didn't. If you don't believe me, try running around making noise and playing like the others did while you were gone. Maybe the big fire will return."

Although the parents were distraught and sad, they did as the boy had suggested. They started playing and making noise in the house, but before that, they prepared a big pot of boiling whale oil and put it at the entrance to the house.

The orphan boy went outside, and once again, he saw a big, red, fiery glow approach from the sea. He ran inside and told the grown-ups, who just carried on playing. But when the monster from the great fire appeared at the entrance tunnel to the house, they tipped the big pot of boiling whale oil over it—and that was how they killed the monster.

Even though the monster was now dead, people continued to be scared that it had the dangerous power to attract, so they threw a piece of wood at it. And quite right: the wood stayed stuck to the monster's dead body. At this point everyone wanted to get outside, but it was difficult to get out of the entrance tunnel without touching the monster. People then crawled out on the wood on the monster's body, and in that way, they were able to get in and out without touching the monster itself.

Finally, only an old woman was left. As she balanced along the wood, a corner of her sealskin clothing accidentally brushed against the monster and immediately got stuck. The woman tore at it, but she couldn't free herself, and suddenly she slipped and landed on her bottom on the monster. Now she was hopelessly stuck, although the others tried to pull and tear her off.

"Try saying, '*Katu, katu, katu,*' and pull yourself up by your arms like you do to get a qajaq up and across thin ice," the people told her.

The old woman did as they said, and would you believe it—it worked! She managed to wiggle free of the monster and flew out of the house, where she landed on the dunghill.

The others wanted to help her get up, but she screamed and howled because her bottom, which had been stuck to the monster, hurt so badly.

The others wanted to flee in the umiaq and take the old woman with them, but when she reached the shore and tried to get into the boat, she was turned into a big mussel that fell into the water and sank to the bottom of the sea.

All the mussels we now find in the sea come from this old woman.

THE WHITE BOY

A very long time ago, some men had been hunting all the way up by Kiatak Island. As they travelled home on their dogsleds, they noticed a big ship.

Many of the men had never seen a ship before. They thought it was a small island made from wood, and that the sails were white wings. When the boats that hung on the sides of the ship were lowered to the water with white men onboard, the hunters thought the ship was giving birth to live young.

But it turned out that the white men were the hostile kind, and so a fierce battle ensued between the Inuit and the white men.

The Inuit won the battle, partly because the white men were unable to stay upright on the slippery ice, while the Inuit had tied the rough skin from the roofs of seals' mouths to the soles of their *kamiit*, which allowed them to run on the ice without falling over.

After the battle, Inuit climbed the ship and discovered many strange things onboard. They saw a big wooden chest, which they dragged ashore.

When they opened it, they found a small, terrified white boy inside it. The boy had been hidden there so he wouldn't be killed in the fight with the Inuit.

The man who found the chest had a little boy of his own, and he took in the white boy.

The two boys grew up together like brothers, and the white boy turned out to be brilliant at catching ravens, which he would give to his foster brother.

The white boy was brought up as an Inuk and learned to hunt with the other children from the settlement.

But every night when the setting sun coloured the sky red, the boy would fall quiet from homesickness, and every now and then he would babble about milk, cakes, and other sweet things that he had been used to eating in the country of the white people.

One day after he had been out hunting, he didn't come back.

They looked for him for a long time but only found some of his clothes in a pile on the ice.

Everyone agreed that his homesickness had made him fly through the air, back to the country from which he had originally arrived on the big ship.

His foster brother missed him very much and would go down to the shore every night to look across the sea.

He hoped that his friend and brother would return one day.

But he never did.

THE LITTLE ORPHANS

Once upon a time, there were two little orphan boys who went ptarmigan hunting every day. They only had their bows and arrows with which to kill the birds.

The people in the settlement really liked the delicious ptarmigan the boys caught, and the boys were happy to share them with the others.

One day the boys went ptarmigan hunting as usual, but caught nothing. On their way home they crossed some tall, steep mountains. From there they could see into a gorge, where they spotted something that looked like it had been built by people.

They made their way down the mountainside and discovered a small house. There were no people to be seen outside, so they climbed onto the roof of the house and looked through the air hole.

There they saw a small boy sitting on the floor playing with a piece of wood as a qajaq and a *kammiut* stick as a paddle.

One of the boys spat out a big glob of saliva near the child. When the little boy saw it hit the floor next to him, he looked up, but the two boys quickly pulled back. Soon they were peering down at him again and saw that the little boy had gone back to playing with his qajaq as before. Then the second boy spat. This time the spit hit the boy's paddle, the kammiut stick.

The little boy started to cry and crawled towards the back of the room.

The two boys went into the house and tried to comfort him.

"Are you home alone?" they asked him.

He nodded and said:

"My mother went out this morning as usual, and she hasn't come back yet."

"We've come to play with you so you don't have to be on your own," the boys said.

Upon hearing this, the boy ventured back onto the floor. The three children played together, but in the afternoon the little boy went outside to look for his mother.

Meanwhile, the two other boys looked around the small house, whose walls were covered with white and blue fox skins.

Finally, the little boy came in and said:

"She's coming. I can see her."

They looked out of the window and saw a big woman, who was carrying something heavy on her back, approaching the house. She was so big the boys thought she must be an inland dweller. They heard a thud outside the house when she dropped the animals she had caught.

The mother came inside, warm and sweaty from carrying her heavy catch.

"Thank you for keeping my little boy company while I was out. It always makes me sad to have to leave him home alone when I go hunting," she said.

Then she turned to her son.

"Have you given them anything to eat?"

"No," the boy said.

The mother went to fetch some dried fox and caribou meat, and a big portion of blubber for the boys.

The two orphans looked at one another because they had never tasted fox meat before, but once they tried a little bit and discovered it was delicious, they gobbled down the food and ate until they were full to bursting.

As they sat there having a nice time, the little boy whispered something to his mother.

"He really wants one of your arrows. That small one there," she said, pointing to one of the arrows.

As a thank you for the food, they gave him one of their arrows, and the little boy was overjoyed.

It had grown dark outside, and the mother suggested they stay the night. They said they would like to do that, and she made up a bed for them near the window.

"You're safe to lie down to sleep now," she said.

And that's what they did.

The next morning as they got ready to leave, the mother paid them for the arrow with a portion of dried meat so big they could barely carry it.

"But don't get anyone else to come here to sell arrows," she said.

Back at the settlement, people had been worried because the two little ptarmigan hunters hadn't come home the night before, so they were delighted to see them. And all the meat they brought back was cause for great joy as well.

"Where have you been?" the people wanted to know.

"We visited people who weren't real," the children said.

The people tasted the dried fox meat and thought it was wonderful.

"We got that as payment for one of our arrows," the two boys said.

"Then let's make a lot of arrows and go there to sell them," the people said.

"No, you mustn't," the two boys said. "Just as we left, the mother told us not to get anyone else to go there and sell arrows."

But the people from the settlement ignored them. The next day they made lots of arrows, and off they went to sell them. The two little boys didn't want to go with them but were forced to do so in order to show them the way.

When they reached the gorge in the mountains, they couldn't see the house, and when they reached the spot where it had been, there was absolutely no trace of it. Nor was there any trace of the woman and the little boy.

Ever since that day, the two little orphan boys never went ptarmigan hunting again.

THE ONE-EYED INLAND DWELLER ON MOUNT KINGITTOQ

Once, in the old days, there was great hunger and suffering in the settlement by Illuerunneq.

People were so weak and exhausted that all they could do was lie on their benches. No one was able to stand up.

No one except one—a small orphan boy. Every day he would go hunting, trying to catch something that the people from his settlement could eat.

If he caught a ptarmigan, he would share it with everyone at the settlement. If he caught two, people were just as happy as if he had caught two seals. True, there was very little flesh on the birds, but at least it meant the people had something for their dried-out tongues to taste.

One day he went hunting. He walked and he walked all day long, but he didn't catch anything. When it began to grow dark, he had reached Mount Kingittoq. He climbed to the very top of it without seeing a single ptarmigan. But although it was almost dark now, he didn't dare return to the settlement without something for the people to eat.

Suddenly he spotted a house. He was very surprised because there had never been a house there before. He walked up to the house, looking about him very carefully as he did so. As the place appeared deserted, he crept through the entrance tunnel to the house. Perhaps he could spend the night there.

An inland giant was sitting inside the house. He had a human body but only one eye.

They were equally surprised to see one another, but the boy was also frightened, because he had heard about inland dwellers who stole children to use them as toys.

"I bet you could do with something to eat, am I right?" the giant said in a friendly voice. "Just sit down."

He went out and came back with plenty of dried meat.

"Eat as much as you like," he said.

The boy ate and he ate. When he couldn't eat any more, the meat pile hadn't dwindled, it was so big.

"You're welcome to stay here tonight. Tomorrow when you're rested, you can go home. You don't have to worry, just lie down and go to sleep. I'll look after you," the inland dweller said.

The boy wasn't sure whether he could trust him, but he was so exhausted and weak that he fell asleep the moment he lay down on the bench.

The next morning as he got ready to leave, the giant gave him a big pile of dried caribou meat to take home to the starving people at his settlement.

The boy was deeply grateful and a little ashamed at having been so suspicious of the giant.

"When you get home, you must tell the people from your settlement under no circumstances to eat blubber with the meat, even if they really want to. Not even a tiny little bit. If they do, you'll never be able to find me again, no matter how hard you look, but if they can restrain themselves, you'll always be able to find me when you need help."

The boy went home, and everyone was surprised and delighted when they saw how much meat he had brought back. He told them what the inland dweller had said and everybody obeyed the order, although there were a couple of old women who muttered something about how lovely it would have been to have a little bit of blubber with the dried meat. When the others heard them, they scolded them and said that the old women should be grateful to have so much good food to eat.

Some days later, the boy returned to the giant. He found the house and was welcomed even more warmly than the first time.

Under the bench he saw a giant rib with plenty of lovely fat.

"I caught a big mammoth," the giant said, pointing to the rib.

The boy didn't know what a mammoth was.

"Sometimes it gets a little dull up here. Not much happens," the giant said. "You're welcome to stay the night."

The boy now trusted the giant, so he decided to stay.

That evening the giant began putting on a shaman suit.

"There's going to be a big *angakkuq* celebration near Equutit. There will be lots of shamans. I'm going—and so are you."

Now, Equutit was a long way away, so the boy didn't fancy the sound of that.

"We'll get there before dawn," the giant reassured him when he saw the anxious look on the boy's face.

So the boy agreed.

While the giant got ready, he told the boy what to do.

"You need to hold on to my neck and close your eyes. You mustn't open them, because you'll get so dizzy that you'll throw up and risk falling off."

They walked to the top of Mount Kingittoq. The boy climbed onto the giant's back and gripped his neck. Then he closed his eyes.

He could feel how the giant flapped his arms and moved his body like a bird getting ready to take off—and then they flew.

All the boy could feel was a strong *whoosh*, just like during a storm, then suddenly the giant said:

"We have reached Equutit."

The boy was very surprised. He thought they had only just left.

He opened his eyes a little bit and saw lots of tiny black dots far, far below them. The dots were the houses in Equutit.

The giant started his descent in big circles.

"Can you see the big house with all the lights? That's where the anga-kkuq celebration is taking place," the giant said.

Then he landed right outside the entrance to the big house.

When they entered, everything was ready for the celebration. Great shamans sang and drummed and performed rituals all night long, one after the other. The giant and the boy didn't fly back home to Kingittoq until the early morning.

"I think you need some sleep now," the giant said. "Just lie down and go to sleep. I'll look after you. When you're rested, then you can go home."

The boy lay down on the bench and fell asleep immediately. Later, when he was ready to go back, the giant gave him a big pile of mammoth meat. The boy got as much as he could carry, but on the same condition as the last time—no one must eat blubber with it if they wanted meat from the giant another time.

When the boy came back, everyone was delighted. It was thanks to him that the people from the settlement survived a tough period of starvation.

"Did you catch a caribou?" someone asked him.

"No, the inland giant up at Mount Kingittoq caught a mammoth."

Then he repeated what the giant had said about how no one was allowed to eat even the smallest piece of blubber with the meat.

"If we do as he says, we can have all the meat we need."

People began to eat with great appetite, but again the old women started talking about how wonderful it would be to have a little bit of blubber with it. Those who heard them got angry and shouted at them.

Suddenly, they heard a big bump outside the house. The walls trembled, and the skin covering the windows cracked.

The furious giant was outside. Behind everyone's back, one of the old women had popped a small piece of blubber into her mouth—and ruined everything.

"How ungrateful you are," the giant shouted angrily. "I gave you as much as you wanted, but you couldn't even do one small thing for me. From now on I won't help you ever again, and no one will be able to find my house, no matter how hard they try."

There was a loud *whoosh*—and the giant was gone.

The boy would often walk up to Mount Kingittoq to look for the giant's house, but he never found it again.

There wasn't the slightest trace of it, not even the remains of a peat wall where the house had once stood.

This is the end of the story.

HOW THE FOG CAME TO BE

A long time ago, there was a giant who lived in the North. Everyone at the settlement was scared of him.

Although he was big and strong, he couldn't be bothered to hunt for his own food. Instead, he would stand on the shore when the hunters returned and take most of their catch—seals, fish, and anything else they had caught for their families during the day. But no one dared do anything about it because he was stronger than any of them.

Whenever anyone protested, he would just laugh at them.

"You're too scared to hurt me," he said. "You're all a bunch of sissies."

But there was one person in the settlement who wasn't a sissy. And that was Alasuk. He wasn't a grown man yet, but ever since he was young, he'd had to provide for his mother because his father had died when he was a little boy.

Everyone at the settlement was fond of him. Every day he would go sailing in his qajaq, and every evening he would come home with food for himself and his mother to eat—and every night the giant would be there, stealing most of what he had caught.

Finally, Alasuk had enough. He might not have been very big, but he was very strong.

One night, when everyone was gathered in the settlement's biggest house for a joyous occasion, the giant burst in. As usual, he took most of the food that had been put out while he looked at the people and grinned. They asked him to leave and not to touch the food, but he just ignored them.

Then he saw a beautiful young girl. She was the daughter of one of the hunters. He went up to her and grabbed her.

"Tonight I want a wife," he said, and dragged her off. The girl protested, and the hunter tried to help his daughter, but the giant was too strong.

Suddenly Alasuk jumped up. He walked up to the giant.

"You think you're so strong," he said, looking the giant right in the eye.

The giant was surprised that anyone dared to challenge him, so he let go of the girl, who quickly ran and hid behind her father. Everyone in the house held their breath, terrified about what might happen next. No one had ever stood up to the giant before.

"Let's see who is the stronger here," Alasuk said. "Tomorrow morning we'll meet down by the shore in our qajait. Then we'll see who can sail around the island the fastest."

The giant roared with laughter.

"Hah, a wimp like you," he snorted, but Alasuk carried on gamely:

"If you win, you can have the young girl, but if I win, then you'll leave this settlement and never come back."

The girl was horrified. She didn't doubt for one second that the giant could easily beat the boy.

The giant laughed at Alasuk. Although he thought it was silly to waste his strength on something like that, he didn't want to look foolish, and so he said:

"We'll meet tomorrow morning. You're going to regret this." And then he left the hall.

Alasuk hurried back to his own tent. His mother looked at him anxiously, but Alasuk reassured her. Then he found a piece of wood and carved himself a giant paddle, much bigger than the one the giant usually paddled with.

The next morning, all the people from the settlement gathered by the shore. They feared the worst, and yet they were curious to see how the contest would end. They were all wondering about the big paddle that Alasuk had brought along, but the giant didn't notice anything. He was too busy getting his qajaq ready and mocking the young boy.

The start signal was given.

Alasuk worked hard with his big paddle and was soon quite a distance ahead of the giant's qajaq. He could hear the giant fuming behind him. Alasuk paddled so fast that if he had been using his regular paddle, it would undoubtedly have snapped. His distance from the giant grew greater and greater, and when he had paddled around the island and steered his qajaq ashore, the people who had been waiting in anticipation to see who came first cheered.

Alasuk had done what no one else had dared do—challenge the

giant. And beaten him on top of that. Now the giant would have to leave the settlement.

But it wasn't going to be as easy as that.

Although Alasuk had won, the giant refused to leave. That evening he burst into the biggest house, where the people were celebrating being rid of him. Everyone got scared and pressed themselves up against the wall. Everyone except Alasuk. Once more he stepped up to the giant.

"You cheated this morning," the giant roared at him. "Your paddle was much bigger than mine."

"Yes, and so what?" Alasuk replied. "You're much bigger than me."

"We'll have a rematch tomorrow morning," the giant said and left the house.

"Fine by me," Alasuk called out, but the giant didn't hear him. He was already back in his own tent.

The next morning, everyone was waiting in tense anticipation down by the shore. The battle was ready to begin, but Alasuk appeared to be late.

When he arrived, a hush rippled through the crowd. They couldn't believe their eyes. Alasuk's paddle was no bigger than a seal's whisker. This could only end badly.

"Why is your paddle so small?" the giant wanted to know.

"My paddle might be small, but it doesn't matter. The water in this bay has magic powers, and if I drink it, I become invincible," Alasuk said.

Then he knelt down on the beach and swallowed a single mouthful of the very salty seawater—but he pretended to drink a lot. When the giant saw Alasuk drink, he also knelt down and began drinking big gulps. He drank and he drank. He wanted to be stronger than Alasuk. He drank so much that he finally burst—and from the place where he had been drinking, a dense, foggy cloud appeared, which floated up into the air.

This is how the fog came to be. And that's why there is so much fog along the northern coasts.

MANUTOOQ, WHOSE DAUGHTERS DRIFTED TO AKILINEQ ON AN ICE FLOE

Once upon a time, there was a man called Manutooq. He had two daughters, but no son who could go hunting with him. And yet he caught a lot of food for his family. Although he hunted alone, his house had the biggest winter stores in the settlement.

He mostly caught seals, but when it was caribou season, he would get into the umiaq with his two daughters, row to the bottom of the fjord, and go hunting there.

They would normally row for two days, and when they reached the heart of the fjord, they would set up camp.

There were plenty of caribou, and in order to catch them, the daughters would herd the caribou towards the father, who would be waiting and ready to shoot them.

He would kill the caribou one after the other with his bow and arrow. For two days he shot and killed so many caribou that he and his daughters barely had time to skin them before it grew dark. They spent the next day drying caribou meat so it would keep throughout the winter.

Just before they were about to head home, he shot another couple of caribou so they would have fresh meat when they returned home.

When they sailed home in the umiaq, it was laden with so much dried and fresh meat that it lay deep in the water.

And so, Manutooq's family never wanted for anything, not even during the harshest winters.

One summer, around the time when caribou fur was very good, they went hunting again.

This time Manutooq's wife as well as their two daughters came with him.

They hunted as they usually did. The girls would chase the caribou towards the father, who would shoot them. A few days later the umiaq was laden with air-dried and smoked meat, and the family began to row home.

It was a long trip, and they made several stops along the way. One of the places they stopped was near a lake where they could get fresh water.

When they reached it, they landed the boat, but for some reason Manutooq wasn't his usual self. Perhaps a spirit had possessed him, or perhaps he had gone a little crazy from working too hard hunting, skinning, and drying meat.

He spoke harshly to his daughters:

"Fetch water!"

The daughters rushed off to the other side of the mountain, where the lake was. They thought it odd that their father had spoken to them like that, but decided that he must just be in a bad mood.

As soon as the two girls were out of sight, Manutooq said to his wife:

"Jump into the boat, and let us sail off without them."

His wife looked at him as if he had gone mad. What could he be thinking? She didn't want to get into the boat and sail off without her daughters.

Manutooq took his harpoon, threatened her, and said:

"If you don't get into the boat now, I'll throw this at you!"

The wife was too scared to do anything else, but she was distraught and desperate as she rowed away from the shore.

And when she heard the girls' happy laughter and chatter from farther inland, tears trickled down her cheeks.

When the girls returned to the shore with the water, they saw to their horror that the boat was already far out into the fjord. They screamed and they cried out, but no matter how much noise they made, their parents continued to row, and the boat moved farther and farther away. Finally it was just a little dark dot on the horizon.

The girls started to cry. They didn't understand why their parents had abandoned them, but they had to accept that from now on they would have to fend for themselves.

Then the older sister spotted a small ice floe sloshing around near the shore.

"Come on," she said to her sister. "That can be our boat, let's hope it takes us home."

They jumped onto the ice floe and slowly started drifting towards

the open sea. They held on to one another because there wasn't much room on the small floe. The wind and the current carried them away. They sailed around the headland and some protruding rocks, and after some days they spotted their settlement.

Just as they were looking forward to coming home, a fresh wind started blowing from the shore. The floe drifted outwards, and although the girls screamed at the top of their voices, no one from the settlement heard them or noticed them.

They drifted out to the open sea. The wind grew more forceful, and the waves grew higher. The small ice floe bobbed up and down. The girls clung to one another in order not to fall off. Soon they couldn't see land anywhere—only the enormous sky and the equally enormous sea.

Suddenly their ice floe began to crack, and a small piece broke off. They looked at one another. What if the entire ice floe broke up?

The older girl had an idea. She took off her long hairband and tied it around the remains of the ice floe, and no more pieces broke off.

Shortly afterwards, they drifted into a dense bank of fog. Now they couldn't see the sea or the sky, and they had no idea which way they were going.

When the fog finally dispersed, they could see something dark on the horizon. It was difficult to know if it was giant waves or land.

The closer they got, the more convinced they were that it was land. They slowly drifted towards the coast until the ice floe stranded. Then the older sister said:

"Once we jump ashore, we mustn't look back until we've reached the beach."

First the older sister jumped ashore, with her back to the sea, then the younger.

Once they both had their feet on firm ground, the older sister said: "Now we can turn around."

And they did, and saw that where the ice floe had been, there was just a little bit of foam sloshing on top of the waves.

On the shore, they found many magnificent narwhal tusks. The younger sister was overjoyed and gathered up a big armful of the long, valuable tusks. She couldn't believe her luck. But the older sister said:

"What are you going to do with those? We need food, not narwhal tusks."

"I think our father would be really happy if he could see all these tusks," the younger girl said.

"Never mention him again. He has been so cruel to us. Let's walk around and see if anyone lives here."

Reluctantly, the younger sister left behind all the beautiful tusks, and they started wandering across the land, even though they were exhausted after several days without food or water.

When they had walked for a very long time, they spotted some ravens flying westward. The big sister knew that ravens like living where there are people, so they carried on in the direction the ravens had flown. After some time they could see the sea again, and right down by the shore they also saw a small house.

Outside the house were two qajait and a big pile of meat, but they couldn't see any people. With the last of their strength, they approached the house to look through the window to see if anyone was home.

They could hear deep voices coming from the house, and when they peered inside, they saw two men sitting at opposite ends of the room.

"Let's go inside," the older girl said.

And that's what they did. The men were brothers and delighted to have company. They gave the girls food and soon married them. The older man took the younger sister, and the younger man took the older sister.

The girls now lived with the men. They never went without food because the men were both skilled hunters.

Some time later, the younger sister discovered that she was going to have a baby. Her husband was delighted because he was very fond of children.

She gave birth to a little boy, and the father—well, both of the men, in fact—were so fond of the little boy that they never let him out of their sight, except when they went hunting. As soon as they came back, they would both start playing with him.

One day after the men had been out hunting and were playing with the little boy, the older sister, who was busy skinning seals outside, went back into the house to fetch something.

When she reached the entrance tunnel to the house, she heard her husband say to his older brother:

"If my wife doesn't have a baby soon, I'm going to kill her."

"Yes, you do that," the older brother said.

The girl was so shocked at hearing this that she didn't go inside the house, but hurried back to her sister and said:

"My husband is going to kill me if I don't have a child soon. And your husband thinks that's fine."

The girls were very scared, but carried on with their skinning as if nothing had happened.

For the rest of that evening they said nothing at all—they were that frightened.

The next day after the men had gone hunting in their qajait, the girls talked about what they could do. They decided to flee, but of course they didn't say anything about this to their husbands when they came back. Over the next few days, they prepared for their flight by packing bags with food and leather for kamiit soles.

One day after the men had gone hunting, they decided that the time to flee had come. They put the little boy in an amauti, picked up their bags, and set off the moment they could no longer see the men's qajait.

They walked all day, but around the time when the men would get back with their qajait, they decided it was better to hide than carry on, because their husbands would undoubtedly come looking for them.

They found a crack in a rock they could squeeze into—and it didn't take long before they could hear their husbands' voices.

As they sat there, they heard one of the men say:

"It was stupid not to kill them immediately. Perhaps they're not real people."

The other man agreed.

When the men came close to the crack in the rock, the girls were scared that they would be discovered. One placed a hand over the mouth of the child so he wouldn't give them away, and they sat as quiet as mice themselves. But fortunately, both men jumped right over the crack in the rock and carried on searching.

The girls breathed sighs of relief but didn't dare crawl back out, because the men would undoubtedly come back the same way when they gave up their search. So they stayed where they were.

When it started to get dark, they heard the men's voices again, but fortunately the men jumped over the crack in the rock again and continued to their house.

Although it had grown dark, the girls emerged from their hiding place and continued along the path. When dawn broke, they had reached the spot where they had originally drifted ashore, and to their surprise the little ice floe on which they had arrived was sloshing around the water's edge.

"Let us jump onto it again," the older sister said. "This time we mustn't look back either."

And then she jumped without looking back.

It was slightly harder for the younger sister to jump because she had the small boy in her amauti, but she made it—also without looking back.

Just when they had jumped onto the ice floe, a fresh breeze started blowing away from land. The ice floe drifted out to the open sea, and soon they could no longer see the coastline.

And so, they drifted for a few days, but this trip was easier because this time they had brought food.

Then they spotted land on the horizon. When they came closer, they could see that they had drifted to a spot a little north of their old settlement.

When they had jumped ashore, the older sister said:

"Now we can turn around."

They both did, and just like the last time, they saw only a little blob of foam bobbing on the top of the waves.

They decided to walk to their old settlement to see if their parents were still alive.

Once they arrived, they could see that their parents' house was still standing.

"That means they're probably still alive," the younger sister said, but they couldn't see any people.

When they reached the entrance tunnel to the house, they couldn't agree which one of them would go in first. After all, it had been such a long time since they had last seen their parents, and what would they say to them? They were also still angry with their parents for abandoning them.

Finally the younger sister crawled in with the baby in her amauti.

Their parents were inside the house. They were very surprised when they heard voices. They weren't used to visitors. They wondered who it could be.

They were even more surprised when they discovered that the visitors were their own daughters.

They had thought that their daughters had died a long time ago—but here they were, and with a baby!

This time their wicked father didn't chase them away, but welcomed them with open arms.

"But where have you been?" their mother wanted to know.

And then the girls told her about the ice floe, about the sea, about the men, about the house, about the child, and about their escape.

The parents were overjoyed to have their daughters back and completely forgot that they had themselves chased them away and caused them to have all these dreadful experiences.

They were also delighted to have a little grandson. They had never expected to have that.

One evening the younger daughter also told them about all the narwhal tusks they had found on the shore.

When Manutooq heard that, he could think of nothing else. He lined the umiaq with three layers of skin, because the sea they would have to cross to reach the shore of Akilineq was very big.

One day when the weather was really nice, he said to his family:

"Get ready. We're going to get the narwhal tusks."

They rowed and they rowed, and when the outer layer of skin got heavy and waterlogged, he cut it off along the stitches and threw it away.

He had to cut off the second skin as well, but when only the innermost layer was left, they saw land and sailed towards it.

When they arrived, they saw the whole shore was covered with narwhal tusks. Manutooq picked up as many as he could fit in the umiaq.

And when they had gathered enough skin to line the boat with three layers again, they sailed home with all the tusks.

Manutooq soon turned into an old man only waiting for death. When he couldn't go hunting any longer, his grandson took over. In the meantime, the boy had grown into a big and strong hunter, who could provide for his whole family.

THE MAN OF THE MOON

Once upon a time, there was a man whose name was Manguaraq, and he was very strong. He wasn't scared to fight any animal and would go up against even the most dangerous bears and whales.

When it was the season for narwhals to swim along the coast, he would go hunting and always come home with food.

One day he came across a big pod of narwhals. As always, he singled out the biggest male in the pod and got ready to throw his harpoon at it. But this narwhal was different. It was white and had a big black spot on its side, just behind its front flippers.

Once Manguaraq had spotted this whale, he no longer wanted to catch anything else. He became a man possessed. However, every time he was about to throw his harpoon, another narwhal would swim in between him and the white whale. Eventually he was forced to give up because it was getting dark, and for want of anything else, he threw his harpoon at an ordinary narwhal.

That night he told his family what he had seen. His old father grew very worried.

"I'm glad you didn't kill it. A white narwhal with a black spot belongs to the Man of the Moon. If you had succeeded, the Man of the Moon would have stolen your soul away. If you ever see this special whale again, you must leave it alone."

Manguaraq ignored his father. He was still obsessed with the white narwhal with the black spot, and the next morning he went hunting again with this one idea in his mind: to catch the white narwhal. He looked for it all day, and although he came across other pods of narwhals, he didn't catch any of them because he only wanted the big white one with the black spot.

Late that afternoon he discovered another pod of narwhals, and there he saw the big white whale he had been searching for all day. When it got close enough for him to hit it, he threw his harpoon and killed it. Then he tied it to his towline and paddled back to the settlement with the big, heavy narwhal.

His old father was standing on the shore waiting for him. From a great distance he saw his son arrive and realized he must have caught a big animal because he was paddling very slowly.

When Manguaraq got closer to the coast, his father could see that his son had killed the big, white male narwhal with the black spot.

"You should have listened to me," his father said when Manguaraq had come ashore. "The Man of the Moon will be angry now. He'll want revenge, so you'd better prepare yourself."

They began cutting up the white narwhal, and when it grew dark, his father said that they should light all the lamps and leave some of them in the entrance tunnel to the house to make sure that everywhere was lit up.

Everyone was afraid of what would happen. The only one who wasn't scared was Manguaraq. Or at least he pretended not to be scared. He took the long, twisted tusk from the narwhal and started carving it.

Night came. Sometimes the sky would be clouded, and at other times there was bright moonlight. They could see a faint glow in the distance, but nothing appeared to be happening. It wasn't until the morning that they heard squeaking footsteps in the snow and a voice thundering:

"I know you're in there, you who killed my prey. No man may hunt my animals. Stop pretending you're not in there. Come outside and let us have a test of strength."

Manguaraq ignored him and continued to carve his tusk.

The voice grew louder and angrier:

"You come outside now, or I can't answer for the consequences. Come outside and show me how strong you are."

Manguaraq continued to ignore the voice, but his father said:

"You asked for this. Go outside and take responsibility for what you have done. You can't expose all of us to danger."

Finally Manguaraq got up, put down the tusk, and quickly got dressed. Then he went outside. His father could see that he was ready to fight the Man of the Moon, and he was sure that very soon he would no longer have a son.

When Manguaraq went outside, he saw the Man of the Moon

standing on an ice floe near the shore. In his hand he held a big *tooq*, an ice drill.

Manguaraq grabbed his own tooq and walked down to the water's edge.

They stood for a while, sizing one another up.

Then the Man of the Moon called out:

"A long time ago, when I was a little boy and I killed my first sparrow chick with a rock, I was shaking with excitement and eagerness to hunt, just as much as I am now."

He raised his tooq and slammed it into the ice, sending large shards of ice flying around him.

Manguaraq wielded his tooq likewise and shouted back:

"When I was a little boy and I had caught my first redpoll bird, I too was shaking with excitement and eagerness to hunt, just as much as I am now."

Then he also slammed his tooq into the ice, sending shards flying.

Then they boasted about who had killed the biggest birds and who had caught the biggest fish.

Manguaraq called out:

"I remember the first catfish I landed in my boat. It had a giant jaw and needle-sharp teeth."

The Man of the Moon raised his tooq again, but without the same force as the last time. Then he called out:

"When I was a little boy, I went fishing. When some women in the boat landed a big catfish and I looked into its giant jaw and saw its shiny, sharp teeth, I got scared and ran to the far end of the boat. You've won this battle because you killed a creature that frightens me. Therefore, I'm inviting you on a trip to the moon."

The Man of the Moon came ashore and started talking to Manguaraq as if the two men were the best of friends.

Manguaraq's father had been almost too scared to leave the house. He was afraid that he would be picking up his son's body after the fight with the Man of the Moon, but to his astonishment, he saw Manguaraq chatting with the Man of the Moon as if they were old friends.

He couldn't believe his own eyes.

The Man of the Moon and Manguaraq flew off, side by side. After they had been flying for some time, they could see land and tall mountains ahead.

When they were close to that land, the Man of the Moon said:

"Once we reach those mountains, you'll experience something that is strange, but also quite funny. The mountain spirit will come out to meet us with a small wooden tray. On this tray there will be a curved knife. The mountain spirit will keep calling out to us: 'Look at the back of my trousers. Holes at the front and holes at the back, and fish hanging out of them. Ha-ha.' It'll shout that to us over and over, but you must be very careful not to laugh at it. Indeed, don't even think about laughing or it'll gut your stomach with its knife and you'll never leave this place."

They heard the mountain spirit hollering before they even reached the mountains:

"Look at the back of my trousers. Holes at the front and holes at the back, and fish hanging out of them. Ha-ha," it laughed hysterically.

The mountain spirit flew close to them while it kept calling out and following them. But although it looked ridiculous, and although its trousers really did have lots of holes, both at the front and at the back, and fish were trying to get out of the holes, Manguaraq had no desire to laugh. He wanted to get safely home from this trip, so he took great care to keep a straight face.

When the mountain spirit realized that Manguaraq wasn't going to fall for its trick and laugh, or crack even a tiny smile, it gave up and flew back inside the mountain, and they heard its maniacal laughter grow fainter and fainter.

Manguaraq and the Man of the Moon flew on and soon reached a small house. The Man of the Moon entered first and Manguaraq followed. Once inside, Manguaraq realized that half the room was cordoned off and completely dark.

The Man of the Moon and Manguaraq sat down on a bench, and the Man of the Moon said:

"Travelling makes you hungry and tired. I think we need something to eat."

No one else was there, but suddenly a young woman appeared from the cordoned-off dark half of the room. She was so beautiful that

Manguaraq couldn't help staring at her, but when she turned to leave, he could see that her back was a skeleton. She soon returned with the most delicious food for them: *maktaaq* from narwhal and dried caribou meat with plenty of fat. A proper feast.

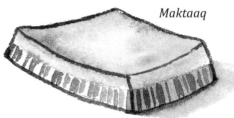

Maktaaq

Then the young woman disappeared into the dark half of the room again, and Manguaraq and the Man of the Moon fell on the food, because they were very hungry by now. Manguaraq didn't eat all that much maktaaq because he'd had plenty of that at home; however, he did eat lots of caribou meat and fat. While they sat there next to each other on the bench, the Man of the Moon told him a story.

"A very long time ago, we lived down on the earth, just as you do. We were a big group of young people who shared a house. We would often play hide-and-seek in the dark. We would blow out all the lamps, walk around, and pick a girl with whom we would lie. When we lit the lamps again, we would discover which girl we had slept with. Sometimes it was very awkward. Once I found a girl I really liked, but when the lamps were lit again, I realized that I had slept with my own sister. She was very embarrassed when she found out. Her face turned bright red and she wanted to run away. On her way out, she grabbed some peat, dipped it in whale oil from the lamp, and lit it in order to light her way. I wanted to run after her, so I also took some peat, but when I tried to light it, it would only glow faintly. When I came outside, she was already gone. Ever since then I've been chasing my sister, but I have never caught her. My sister is the Sun, and we live in the same house, but when my half is light, her half is dark, and vice versa."

Manguaraq listened to the Man of the Moon's story. Now he had learned why the Sun and the Moon are never seen together.

They had a great time. The Man of the Moon told more stories while he carved a narwhal tusk, and then suddenly they heard the mountain spirit cackle outside the window. It would appear he had not given up hope he could make them laugh at his trousers. He tried to get into the house, pushing his little wooden tray with the curved knife in front of him. The Man of the Moon got so angry that he kicked aside the tray, sending it flying. The curved knife fell to the ground.

"That's no way to treat our guest. Get out of here," the Man of the Moon said.

Again, the mountain spirit gave up trying to make Manguaraq laugh. They heard his cackle disappear into the distance.

At this point the Man of the Moon had produced a small pile of shavings from the tusk. He gathered them together and stood up. Manguaraq thought this was in order to chuck them outside, but instead he opened a small hatch in the floor and called for Manguaraq.

Manguaraq found himself looking down at the earth and all the little houses down there. The Man of the Moon took the tusk shavings and scattered them across the earth. A moment later, the ground was completely covered with snow. The Man of the Moon said:

"That's how I cover the earth in deep snow when people don't behave properly. It gives them something to think about."

Then they both lay down on the bench to sleep, and the next morning, when Manguaraq said that he would like to go home, the Man of the Moon followed him on his way to make sure Manguaraq wasn't bothered by the mountain spirit again.

When Manguaraq returned to his settlement, his father was overjoyed. When his son and the Man of the Moon had flown off the day before, his father had never expected to see him again.

And that is the story of how the Man of the Moon forgot his anger and how the skilled hunter Manguaraq saved himself.

THE WOMAN WHO MARRIED A PRAWN

Once upon a time, there was a man who had a very beautiful wife. Their daughter was even more beautiful—a true beauty. Young men from their own and neighbouring settlements came to ask if she wanted to marry them, but she said no to all of them. She insisted she didn't want to get married.

Now, this made her parents a little sad, because they wanted their daughter to get herself a husband—partly because they would gain a son-in-law who could get food for them when the father became too old to go hunting.

One evening they heard a strange noise. It sounded almost like laughter:

"*Hua, hua, hua.*"

The sound was coming from the daughter's place on the bench. The parents looked over there, but the daughter had hung up a curtain made from skin so they couldn't see her.

The next morning they asked what it was they had heard, and she said that she had married a giant prawn.

Her parents wanted to meet their new son-in-law, but the prawn refused to show himself to anyone else in the house. He stayed behind the skin curtain.

When winter came, it became difficult to go sailing and catch food. People from the settlement went hungry—the caches were empty, including in the girl's house. Her father grumbled about having a son-in-law who couldn't help them get food, especially when he thought of all the young, strong hunters who would have liked to marry his daughter. The parents dearly wished that their daughter had taken one of them instead.

One day there was a terrible snowstorm. You would risk your life going outside. The wind was howling and the snow was lashing down. Suddenly the family heard what sounded like wild drum dancing through the roar of the storm, and a moment later, three big common seals were thrown into the entrance tunnel to the house.

No one in the house could believe their own eyes. Seals at this time of winter, and in a snowstorm like this one—how was that possible?

The daughter walked over to the seals and asked her mother to skin them so they could all have something to eat. Then she said that it was her husband, the prawn, who had taken human form and gone hunting to provide food for his family.

It is said that all animals can assume human form, and that was what the prawn had done.

There was much joy in the house at the prospect of food. Everyone was weak and exhausted because they hadn't had anything to eat for a long time.

When the mother had skinned the seals, the daughter said that everyone could help themselves to as much meat as they wanted.

"But save the bottom bit of the ribs for my husband. He would like that piece."

That piece was set aside for the prawn, and they made a feast out of the rest of the seals.

From then on, the prawn went hunting every single day, and every day he brought meat back to the family. They had never had so much food during winter.

Some time later, the girl discovered that she was expecting a baby. However, she ended up having not just one but two lovely boys who brought joy to the whole house. No one had yet seen their father. He never appeared to anyone other than the daughter.

One evening the parents heard sounds from the daughter's place on the bench. Chatting and laughter. And again, this peculiar laughter:

"*Hua, hua, hua.*"

The mother-in-law was very curious. She thought it strange that she had never seen her daughter's husband and the father of the twin boys. She tiptoed over to the sealskin curtain that the daughter had hung up to have some privacy with her husband.

The mother peeked through a hole in the skin and saw her son-in-law for the first time. The prawn had assumed human form and was sitting in the middle of the bench laughing out loud with his strange laughter. But what a sight he was: a small man with skinny arms and legs, and eyes that stuck out of his head.

When the mother-in-law saw her daughter's husband, she was so shocked that she dropped dead on the spot.

So, you could say that the daughter's husband killed his mother-in-law—without even wanting to.

After that incident, no one ever dared spy on the daughter and her husband. They looked after themselves and their two little boys, and they were fine. And the son-in-law continued to bring plenty of food back to the house.

And that was the story about the woman who married a prawn.

ALLUNNGUAQ, WHO WAS TEASED BY THE PEOPLE FROM HIS SETTLEMENT

Once upon a time, there was a young man whose name was Allunnguaq. His father was dead, so Allunnguaq had to provide for his mother and his younger brother.

Unfortunately, he was no great hunter. When the men went seal hunting in the summer, Allunnguaq would usually come home without having caught anything at all. The other hunters couldn't help teasing him, and when they approached the shore in the evening, having been out hunting all day, they would call out to Allunnguaq's younger brother:

"Allunnguaq has caught a seal. Allunnguaq has caught a seal."

Allunnguaq was always one of the last to come home, and his younger brother would wait by the shore to help him with the seal— only to be disappointed time and time again, until he realized that the men were just playing a trick on him. Then he stopped waiting.

But one summer, something strange happened: Allunnguaq suddenly became a very successful hunter. He began bringing home several seals most nights. His luck lasted late into the autumn.

The other hunters from the settlement grew jealous and said:

"Allunnguaq will soon have caught all the seals he's allowed in his lifetime. So he'll probably die soon."

The frost and the cold came early that year, and people in the settlement were already starving in late autumn.

In the settlement lived a famous hunter and shaman whose name was Qilaassuaq. But even in his house there was starvation and suffering. People were so faint from hunger that they didn't have the strength to go hunting.

Allunnguaq was the only one to still go hunting, although there wasn't a lot to catch.

He went out on the frozen sea looking for holes in the ice where the seals would come up to breathe. There weren't many of them, but when he finally found one, he marked it by peeing on the ice nearby so he would be able to find it again.

But no seals appeared, so Allunnguaq gave up hunting on the ice and instead went up into the mountains to catch ptarmigan. Perhaps his chances of finding something he could bring back to the people from his settlement would be better there.

Whenever he caught a ptarmigan, his mother would skin it as if it had been a seal. And although there wasn't much meat on a small ptarmigan, it would still be shared with every house in the settlement.

Then the snow came. It snowed and it snowed—so much that the people could barely leave their houses. Allunnguaq put a tent pole right outside his house, and using that, he could gauge how deep the snow was. Finally, he could only see the top of the pole. When it stopped snowing at long last and the weather grew pleasant again, people were unable to go outside. They had to wait for the snow to compact so they could walk on it.

This took many days, and during all that time they had nothing to eat.

When the snow was finally strong enough to support his weight, Allunnguaq went outside the house. But he was the only one who could walk. Everyone else from the settlement was so weak they couldn't move.

He went back inside and said to his mother and younger brother:

"Today I want to go to that hole I marked out on the ice."

His family waited for him to come back with a catch, but much time passed and he didn't come home. When it was almost dark, his mother went outside and sat on the roof of the entrance tunnel to the house. She looked across the ice and suddenly noticed Allunnguaq in the distance. He was pulling something, but because of all the snow and the poor light, she couldn't see what it was.

This time it was Allunnguaq himself who called out towards the shore:

"I've caught a seal."

Allunnguaq's mother was so proud and happy, and she called out to the others in the settlement:

"Allunnguaq has caught a seal. Allunnguaq has caught a seal."

There was joy in every household, but many people were so emaciated from hunger that they couldn't join in the cheering.

Allunnguaq's mother dragged the seal into the house and cut it up. Then she gave all the people in the settlement a small piece of skin to chew on, a portion of blubber, and some meat.

Over five days, Allunnguaq caught five seals from the same breathing hole in the ice. The meat was shared among everyone in the settlement.

Qilaassuaq the shaman sent a message to Allunnguaq asking him not to throw away the seal bones. During times of starvation, they could always gnaw on them—just like the dogs did.

After those five seals, Allunnguaq didn't catch any more from the breathing hole, although he would often go there. So he went ptarmigan hunting on the mountain instead, but he had no luck there, either.

One day when he was in the mountains, he saw blow from a whale in the distance. It meant there had to be a stretch of open water.

That night he told his mother—and only her—that he would head out to see if there were any eider ducks trapped in the hole.

He gathered his hunting kit, and very early the next morning, while everyone was still asleep, he set out.

He hadn't come back when it grew dark that evening, so his mother and younger brother began to worry that something might have happened to him. His younger brother wanted to go down to the sea to look for him, but his mother said he had to go to bed. She, too, went to bed, but she couldn't fall asleep.

Later that night, she heard squeaking footsteps in the snow. It was Allunnguaq coming home. Then she heard him drop something very heavy as he called out:

"Mother, please would you give me a hand?"

His mother got up, put on her kamiik, and went outside.

In the darkness she could see the outline of a big animal.

"What have you caught?" she said.

"I found an opening in the ice where narwhals were trapped," Allunnguaq said.

His mother helped him lug the heaviest narwhal inside the house so she could skin it. Then she said to the younger brother:

161

"Go to the other houses and tell them Allunnguaq has caught an animal with strong blood that will make a good and powerful soup. Tell them they can come here to eat."

The younger brother hurried around to all the houses, bringing joy wherever he went.

Only Qilaassuaq the shaman didn't believe him. He said:

"Allunnguaq would never be able to catch an animal as big as a narwhal. He could barely catch a seal."

But when the younger brother showed him a piece of maktaaq from the narwhal, Qilaassuaq reached out for it as he cried:

"Give it to me. Give it to me."

He snatched the maktaaq from the younger brother and ate it all himself, even though it was meant for everyone in the house.

Many of those who lived in the settlement were so weak from starvation that they couldn't stand up, so Allunnguaq's mother brought them meat and maktaaq.

When the people had recovered some of their strength, several of the men walked with Allunnguaq to the opening in the ice to catch the rest of the trapped narwhals and bring them back to the settlement.

And so it was that Allunnguaq, whom everyone had mocked and teased, saved all the people in his settlement from starving to death.

And this is the end of the story.

TUSILARTOQ, WHO WAS BORN TOO SOON

Singajik, the hunter, and his wife, Marnilik, had travelled far north to Niaqunngunaq with many other people from their settlement to go caribou hunting.

Marnilik was expecting a baby, but it wasn't due for a very long time.

They had pitched their tents by a bay in the fjord, and Singajik and most of the other men had headed far into the mountains to hunt caribou. They were gone for several days, and when Singajik eventually returned to his tent after a good hunt, his wife was poorly. Her stomach hurt, and during the night it grew worse and worse. The baby was being born, even though it was a long time before it was supposed to.

Singajik told one of the women in their tent to visit every tent at the campsite to see if anyone knew anything about childbirth.

First the woman went to the tent farthest away. Two old women lived there, but they both said they knew nothing about childbirth. It was so long since they'd had children themselves.

"But there's someone in the southern tent who usually helps out with things like that," they said.

The woman rushed to the southernmost tent, where an old woman lived. The woman asked her if she could help with the birth, and she said that she could.

"I've often helped bring children into the world. I'd be happy to help."

They hurried back to Singajik's tent, where Marnilik was in a lot of pain. The old woman took off her kamiik and sat down on the bench behind Marnilik. She sat there for a long time, helping with the birth. Finally, after much time had passed, she said:

"Marnilik has had a little boy, but he's very small and weak, and I'm not sure he'll survive. Do you have any clothes for him?"

Marnilik said:

"I hadn't expected the baby to come for a long time, so I didn't bring

anything, but just before we left the settlement, my mother gave me a bag of eider duck skins. Perhaps the biggest of those will fit him."

One of the women went to fetch the bag. When they opened it, they saw it was full of the softest eider duck skins. They found the biggest and gave it to the midwife. She dressed the little boy in it, and it fit him exactly once they stuck his little arms out where the bird's wings used to be. Then she took another skin and put it over the first one so he wouldn't be cold. Now the little boy looked almost like an eider duck— he was no bigger than that—and the midwife handed him to his mother so he could drink some milk from her breast.

Then the midwife put on her kamiik and got ready to leave, but before she left the tent, she said:

"I don't know if he'll survive, but I've left a tiny feather on his lips. Watch it carefully—as long as it's moving, then he's breathing, and that means he's still alive."

Marnilik put the little boy to her breast, but he couldn't work out how to suckle at all. The tiny feather on his lips kept fluttering, but he was born so early that he wasn't fully developed. He didn't even have any fingernails.

They tried putting some drops of milk onto a mussel shell and moistening his lips with it. He lapped it up, but he couldn't drink.

Both his father and mother were very worried.

It wasn't until three days after the birth that he discovered his mother's breast and started suckling a little, but by then he was so weak that he had almost no strength left.

Marnilik kept offering him her breast, and he slowly got better at suckling. But they didn't take the tiny feather away from his lips until he was really good at drinking, because it wasn't until then that they could be sure he was really alive and breathing.

On the day the little boy was born, Singajik didn't go caribou hunting with the other men. He stayed with his wife and his newborn son. It was, after all, more important than hunting.

Nor did Singajik go hunting on the many other occasions the other men set out—in fact, he didn't go caribou hunting at all for the rest of the summer.

One evening when one of the women from Singajik's tent was walking around the campsite, she heard chatter and laughter coming from some young women by an umiaq.

She went closer to find out why they were giggling, because it sounded as if they were having a really good time. Suddenly, she heard one of the girls snigger:

"I don't know why Marnilik doesn't just let that runt of a baby die. Surely there's no point in keeping him alive."

The woman from Singajik's tent was so shocked to hear the girl talk like that that she didn't want to join the group. She walked back to her tent in silence and sat on her bench just as silently.

After Singajik had gone out in his qajaq to catch seals the next day, Marnilik asked her:

"What's wrong with you? You're not your usual self. Are you missing the settlement?"

"It's because I heard something yesterday that made me really sad," the woman said.

"You shouldn't bottle up things that make you sad," Marnilik said.

So the woman told her what the young women had been chatting about down by the umiaq the night before.

"It made me so sad," the woman said. "I thought it was a nasty thing to say. We're so happy to have this baby, and we're doing everything we can to keep him alive—why would they say something like that?"

When Marnilik heard that, she also fell very quiet.

When Singajik came back that evening, his wife was quiet, but she didn't tell him why.

It wasn't until two days later that she said to him:

"The young girls here at the campsite have been speaking ill about our helpless little boy. They have made fun of him, and they think we should have let him die. I'm going to fast for seven days and hope that the spirits will let him grow and become big and strong."

After six days of eating nothing at all, she said to Singajik:

"Tomorrow it'll be seven days since I last ate. I want you to get me a seal that was killed in salt water so I'll have something to eat when my fast is over."

Singajik wondered where he would go to catch a saltwater seal, because the water near their fjord was mainly brackish, and he didn't know of any places nearby where he could hunt seals. Then he remembered that he had heard someone mention a place out by the mouth of the fjord where there were said to be seals even in the middle of the summer.

The next morning the weather was good, and Singajik decided to seek out the place he had heard of, although it was a long way away.

He paddled and paddled until he finally reached the mouth of the fjord.

He hadn't been waiting for very long before he spotted a common seal. He lay down in his qajaq so the seal wouldn't notice him. He carefully moved close to it in order to throw his harpoon. He threw his harpoon with all his strength and hit the seal. Then he tied it to his towline and began paddling home.

Marnilik had said that no one must touch the seal he had caught except for Singajik himself, and that he must bring it to the tent and place it with its head pointing towards the tent opening.

He didn't return home until late that evening. Many people came down to the shore to help him with the seal, but he told them:

"No one must touch this seal with their hands. You're welcome to help pull it ashore with the towline, but I must be the one to carry it up to the tent."

So that is what they did, and when Singajik had sorted out his qajaq, he grabbed the seal's front flippers and dragged it towards the tent, where he placed it outside with its head facing the opening. Then he flung the flap aside and entered the tent, where his wife was sitting on the bench, breastfeeding their little son.

Singajik sat down next to her and said:

"I've caught a seal that lived in salt water and placed it outside, just like you told me to."

Marnilik handed the little boy to his father, got up and took her *ulu*, skinning knife, and went outside.

Shortly afterwards she returned with the seal and cut the meat into small pieces. She put everything under the bench. Then she put blubber in the lamp and lit it.

The big pot that hung from the tent pole was lowered, filled with water, and placed over the fire. When the water was boiling hot, she took out the meat and cut off a tiny piece of rib gristle and a small piece of gut. She threw them in the water.

After it had boiled for a long time, she fished out the gristle and the intestine and said:

"For the next five days, this will be all that I eat. When those five days have passed, the rest of you may eat what you want of the seal, but not before."

The other caribou hunters at the campsite had shot so many animals that they had filled up the umiat, and therefore, they packed up their tents and returned to the settlement. But Singajik and Marnilik didn't dare travel yet. Their son was still too small and weak to cope with the long journey.

When autumn came and the frost arrived, they finally decided to head back to the settlement.

One day when the air was clear, Singajik studied the sky to see which direction the wind was coming from and whether there was a storm brewing. The outlook was fine, so they packed their tent and their belongings, and Singajik said:

"We don't have to worry about whether he can manage the journey now. He's eating well and has started to grow."

And so they travelled south. They rowed for a whole day, and when the last rays of the sun were disappearing into the sea, they rounded the last headland and could see their settlement. There were already lamps lit in the houses, and Singajik and Marnilik were glad to be home again.

It was almost dark by the time they reached the shore, so no one noticed them, but Singajik called out at the top of his voice:

"Umiaq. Umiaq." And that attracted the attention of everyone at the settlement. People rushed out of their houses and down to the shore, and everyone wanted to know:

"How is your little boy?"

Singajik replied that the boy was well, and everyone was overjoyed.

Singajik and Marnilik returned to their house with their little boy, who continued to grow and gain weight.

Marnilik's mother, who had stayed behind at the settlement while the others went caribou hunting, was delighted to see her first grandchild.

One night when Marnilik was breastfeeding him, Singajik said:

"We were too scared to give him a name until we knew if he would survive. Now that it looks like he'll make it, it's time to think of a good name for him. Is there anyone you or your mother would like to remember and name him after?"

Marnilik thought about this for a long time.

"No," she said. "There's no one in my family I want to name him after, but you're his father—perhaps you have someone you would like to remember?"

"There are many people I would like to remember," Singajik said, "but I think I'll name him after my father, who lived to a ripe old age. And so we'll call him Tusilartoq."

And so it was that the little boy was given his grandfather's name, and like him, the boy grew up to be a great and strong hunter.

THE THUNDER SPIRITS

Once upon a time, two sisters were playing together. However, their father, who wasn't used to children and wasn't very fond of them, soon grew tired of listening to them. He complained that they were making too much noise. Then he shouted at them and told them to go somewhere far away to play.

He would yell at them like that, day in and day out, their entire childhood.

When the girls grew older and started making their own decisions, they decided to run away from home because they couldn't bear to listen to their father's harsh words any longer.

All they took with them was a dog skin, a piece of kamik leather, and a flint stone for starting fires. Then they made their way to a tall mountain to live there.

Their parents searched for them, but the girls hid so no one could find them. They became *qivittut*, hermits living in the mountains who wanted nothing to do with other people.

From time to time they would come across caribou hunters, but the girls didn't want to go back to living with other people.

Life in the mountains was tough, and it was difficult to get enough food, so eventually they starved to death.

When they died, they turned into evil spirits, the kind that make thunder.

When the two evil spirits shook their dry kamik leather, violent thunderstorms would follow. When they struck their flint stone, there would be lightning in the sky, and whenever they peed, it would rain.

Their father met with many shamans trying to get the girls to come back, but when a shaman told him that the girls were dead, he gave up.

It is said that once the girls had turned into evil spirits, they returned to the world of people to haunt them.

They went back to their settlement to take revenge on their parents, who had been so mean to them when they were little. They frightened everyone in their parents' house to death, except an old woman with a small child in her *amaat*, the big hood of her annuraaq.

They let her live so she could tell other people about their strong and evil powers to make other people fear them too.

Whenever the thunder spirits visit, the whole earth trembles in fear—even stones on flat ground will roll towards people.

During thunderstorms, you will hear roaring and crackling, just like the noise you make when you shake a dry piece of leather. The sky will be lit up by sparks from the flint stone the girls carry with them, and the rain will be pouring down. Everything that sticks up into the air can be struck by fire from the lightning. You risk your life going outside.

When the weather is like that, people will nick the ear of a dog with a red coat so it bleeds, then let the dog walk around the house, dripping blood the whole way. By doing that, they ensure their house will be safe against fire. This is because the only thing the thunder girls fear is dogs with red coats.

THE TWINS WHO LEARNED TO DIVE

Once upon a time, there lived a hunter who was skilled at all kinds of sport.

He had no children, and it was his greatest wish to have a son.

"If I had a son, I would teach him all sorts of things," he said.

Whenever he visited different settlements, he would ask the people:

"How can you teach a child to hold its breath underwater for as long as a seal?"

No one could answer his question until he met an old man who said:

"Your wife will have twins, but before they're born, you must prepare. You must fetch some meltwater from the farthest mountains, and you must collect the regurgitated food of a black guillemot. You must also collect what the black guillemots eat. You will find that in the mountains where the birds live. Once the twins are born, the first things they eat and drink must be meltwater from the farthest mountains and the regurgitated food of black guillemots. They must also eat some of what the birds eat. They must have all this before they drink their mother's milk. Then you must hold their heads underwater, and if they can hold their breath for as long as a black guillemot when it dives, then you can train them to be underwater for as long as a seal. As they grow up, they must never eat hot food, they must drink only icy water, and they must never be allowed near fire. Nor must they wear clothes—they should always be naked."

Some time later, the man's wife got pregnant. He was very happy, and when the time for the birth came, he found an old woman who could help. To his enormous joy and surprise, his wife gave birth to twins. Two little boys.

Although the old man had warned him, the new father hadn't prepared, and now he got busy fetching the things the old man had told him to get.

"You mustn't give the children anything to eat until I come home," he said to his wife before he set out in his qajaq.

He didn't take the time to explain to his wife why he was leaving, so she was both angry and sad and concluded he was leaving because he wanted nothing to do with the children.

When the man came back, he brought water from the farthest mountains in his glove, a cod that a black guillemot had regurgitated, and a capelin caught near a mountain where the birds live.

He gave these things to the newborn babies to eat, and then he held their heads underwater. He didn't pull them out of the water until their heads started to shake, and by then they had held their breath for as long as a black guillemot. This made the man very happy. It gave him hope that one day they would learn to be underwater as long as a seal.

He dried the children and placed them at their mother's breast, and it wasn't until then that they had their first taste of milk.

The man trained them every day, and when they were only one month old, they could hold their breath as long as a common seal.

As they grew up, the man made sure to toughen them up. They ate only cold meat and never came near fire or heat. The water they drank was icy, and they were always naked, even when they were outside, even though there was snow and frost.

At times the boys would be gone for many days, and their parents began to worry that something might have happened to them. But they always came back—and their hair was always wet when they did.

One day the father said to them that he and their mother would like to see how skilled they had become at diving.

They walked to a lake. There was a mountain by the lake with a steep slope that reached into the water. The boys climbed it and jumped into the lake from there. A long time passed, and they still couldn't be seen. Their mother started to weep, but when they had been underwater for as long as a hooded seal can be, they returned to the surface.

"Now show us what you'll do to evade an enemy," their father said, and threw a stone at them. The stone hit the exact spot where the boys had just been, but by then they had long since disappeared under the water. This time they were completely gone. Their parents were convinced they had lost their two sons and prepared to go home. But yet again, the boys resurfaced unharmed.

Although he had been very worried, the man was proud of his sons.

"Now you need to learn how to catch seals in the sea," he said, and took them down to the sea. "It's about time you learn how to provide food for the family."

The boys hadn't swum in salt water before. They had practised only in mountain lakes.

When they reached the sea, they climbed onto a protruding rock and jumped from it into the waves.

This time they stayed under for longer than they ever had before. In fact, it was night by the time they came back. They had caught a seal in the water. One boy had spotted it, and then they had followed it for a long time before one of them managed to grab hold of the back flippers. Then the other brother had clubbed it over the head and killed it.

Like that, they had caught their first seal—and after that, many more. Eventually they caught so much food for their family that their father didn't have to go hunting in his qajaq again.

One day when they came home, one boy said that they'd had to turn around because his brother was cold.

This worried the father right away.

"Have you eaten warm meat?" he demanded to know.

"No."

"Have you been near fire?"

"No."

"You must have done one or the other," the father said, "or you wouldn't be cold now."

And then the boy had to admit that he had indeed tasted warm meat. It had looked delicious, and the aroma had been so tempting.

"What a shame," the father said. "Now you can't tolerate being in the water for as long as your brother."

People from other settlements heard about the two boys who were such amazing divers and who could stay underwater for as long as seals.

A message came saying that many qajait from another settlement would arrive to see the boys perform. When the father heard this, he said:

"Many qajait can also mean many enemies. You never know who might turn up. Watch out in case someone arrives who isn't here just to admire you."

A few days later, many qajait arrived, all heading for the settlement. The boys ran to the shore and jumped into the sea.

"Look, there they are," the men in the qajait shouted, and began chasing the boys. It turned out the men hadn't come to admire them, but to kill them, because they were envious they could catch so many seals. When the boys discovered this, they started swimming away from the shore and out towards the open sea, where it was very deep indeed.

Once they were there, the boy who had started to feel the cold said: "I'll create a storm."

Then he dived right to the bottom of the sea. Down there, he found a tube of seaweed and started blowing through it.

When he resurfaced, his brother said:

"Why don't you swim home before you get too cold? I can handle them from now on."

So one brother swam home while the other kept resurfacing in order to entice the qajait even farther out into the open sea.

And then a powerful storm arose. Most of the qajait keeled over, and the men drowned. The boy swam up to the ones that were still afloat, snatched the paddles from them, and upended the qajait, so those men drowned as well. When no more enemies were left alive, he swam ashore.

There, he discovered a single qajaq paddler trying to get away, but he also tipped over his qajaq, and the man drowned.

That is how the boys eliminated all their enemies, and since that day, no one ever dared attack them again.

THE WOMAN WHO TAUGHT HERSELF TO HUNT

Once upon a time, there was a man and his wife who had only one child. The man was a great shaman, and they loved their son very much. But unfortunately, the little boy died.

The parents were distraught and felt terrible—also towards each other—so when the people from their settlement decided to move to a new place, the man went off with the others without taking his wife.

As they sailed away in the umiaq, another woman said to the man:

"Why aren't you taking your wife? You can't just leave her behind all alone."

The man made no reply; he just looked straight ahead and carried on rowing. No one else in the boat said anything. They pretended they hadn't heard the conversation.

The woman who had been left behind in the abandoned settlement was furious with her husband. But she decided she would try to survive on her own.

What her husband didn't know was that she was expecting another child.

She left the settlement and wandered for days until she reached the sea. There she saw a giant whale, which was beached. A seagull was sitting on the dead whale, pecking at the flesh.

The woman chased away the seagull and started cutting big chunks of meat from the whale. All on her own, she carried the heavy pieces of meat a little farther inland. There she built herself a house from the whale's enormous ribs and bones, which she collected from the shore.

She made windowpanes from the whale's guts to let some light into her house.

She gave birth to her baby inside this house when her time had come. It was a little girl.

The baby helped soothe the pain of losing her first child, and the woman did everything she could to make her little daughter happy.

She fetched some seal flippers from the water's edge and made dolls out of them for her daughter.

When winter arrived, foxes started coming right up to the house to eat from her store of whale meat.

So she made some snares from whale sinews in order to catch them. In this way, she caught several foxes. She skinned them and used their skins for bedding so she and the baby could sleep more comfortably. She caught so many foxes that she was able to line the walls and the ceiling with fox skin. And this made her house cozy and warm.

One day when the mother was sewing, the little girl said:

"One of my dolls can move."

"Oh, nonsense," the mother said. "You just play with your dolls."

But the child insisted:

"No, one of my dolls really can move."

A few days later the girl said:

"Mother, one of my dolls is a shaman. It says my father will come tomorrow."

But again, the mother said:

"Don't be silly. You haven't got a father."

But the girl insisted:

"My doll says that once it has grown dark and then light again, my father will come."

But her mother refused to listen to her.

The next morning, they heard strange noises outside. The mother looked out the window and saw a man approach on a sled.

He came right up to the house, stepped off his sled, and entered. Now the mother could see that the man was her husband.

He looked about the house. He was clearly impressed with what he saw.

"How did you manage to catch all those foxes?" he wanted to know.

"With snares I made from whale sinews," she said, and told him how she had found the whale that had provided them with food and building materials for the house.

The man stayed in the house that night, and the next morning he wanted to take the woman and the little girl home to his new settlement.

But the woman refused. She was fine where she was, she said.

Then the man left on his sled, and the woman and the child lived in the house during the winter, eating the rest of the whale meat.

The following spring, the woman decided to go to her husband's new settlement after all. She packed up their things and left with her daughter.

When she reached the settlement, she discovered that her husband had married another woman, but when he saw his first wife and their child, he left his new wife and remarried his first wife.

They lived together for many years, and when the man died, the woman lived on her own with her daughter. She provided for them both—she would go hunting and catch seals, fish, and other animals, so they never went hungry. After all, she had taught herself to hunt when she lived all alone by the sea.

She could do everything on her own.

THE RAVEN AND THE LOON

This is the story of how the raven and the loon—known as the great northern diver—got their colours and patterns.

A long time ago, both birds were white all over. Then one day a raven and a loon met and agreed that they would paint colours and patterns on one another's feathers. The raven went first and started to paint the loon.

It gave the loon plenty of little white and black dots. In some places the dots were very close together, and in other places farther apart. The raven was very pleased with its work and asked the loon if it was pleased also, which it was. Very pleased indeed. It thought its plumage was beautiful—much nicer than when it was completely white.

Now it was the turn of the loon to paint the raven. It took the black colour and painted the raven's feathers so it ended up being black with big, white dots. The dots were the same size and spread in an even pattern all over its body. Just like the raven, the loon was very pleased with its work. It asked the raven what it thought, but the raven wasn't entirely happy. It had discovered that some dots under one of its wings were a little crooked in relation to each other. So it grabbed the black paint and started fixing the loon's work, but it didn't take long before it had painted itself black all over.

When it discovered what it had done, it was very sad and cross with itself. It started screeching:

"*Qaaq, qaaq, qaaq!*"

Now, in our language that's the word for a bench skin—the skin you put on the bench where you sleep. People didn't think that ravens had a voice, so they thought it must be a person calling out. They gathered together and someone said:

"Someone needs a bench skin to sleep on. Fetch one, quickly."

Someone came running with a bench skin and placed it on the ground. But no one came to fetch it—and the raven kept screeching:

"*Qaaq, qaaq, qaaq!*"

And this is how the raven got its never-ending cry, and the loon and the raven their colours and plumage.

Or so the old people tell us.

GLOSSARY

Notes on Inuktitut Pronunciation

There are some sounds in Inuktitut that may be unfamiliar to English speakers. The pronunciations below convey those sounds in the following ways:

- A double vowel (e.g., aa, ee) lengthens the vowel sound.
- Capitalized letters denote the emphasis for each word.
- q is a "uvular" sound, a sound that comes from the very back of the throat. This is distinct from the sound for k, which is the same as a typical English "k" sound (known as a "velar" sound).
- R is a rolled "r" sound.
- ll is a rolled "l" sound.

For additional Inuktitut-language resources, please visit inhabitmedia.com/inuitnipingit.

WORD	PRONUNCIATION	MEANING
Akilineq	a-KI-li-niq	Place name.
amaat	a-MAAT	The back pouch of an annuraaq used to carry a baby.
amauti	a-MOW-ti	A woman's parka with a pouch for carrying a child.
angakkuq	a-ŋak-KOOQ	A shaman.
annuraaq	an-nu-RAAQ	A type of coat with a hood, often made of seal or caribou skin.

Equutit	E-quu-tit	Place name.
iglu	IG-loo	A snow house.
Illuerunneq	Il-LUE-run-neq	Place name.
Ilulissat	i-lu-LIS-sat	Place name.
Inuit	i-NUIT	This means "people" and is used to refer to people indigenous to the Arctic regions.
Inuk	I-nuk	The singular form of "Inuit."
kamiik	ka-MEEK	Two skin boots.
kamik	ka-MIK	One skin boot.
kamiit	ka-MEET	Many skin boots.
kammiut	kam-MIUT	A wooden stick used to soften leather for kamiit.
Kangaarsuk	ka-NGAAR-suk	Place name.
kapussivik	ka-PUS-si-vik	A strap going across the front of a qajaq under which a paddle can be stored to keep from falling over.

Kamiik

185

Nunatak

Kiatak	KIA-tak	Place name.
Kingittoq	KI-ngit-toq	Place name.
Kulusuk	KU-lu-suk	Place name.
maktaaq	MUK-tuk	Pieces of whale skin and blubber. It is regarded as a kind of candy, a great delicacy. It is eaten raw.
Narsaq	NAR-saq	Place name.
Niaqunngunaq	Nnia-QUNG-ngu-naq	Place name.
Noorsiit	NOOR-siit	Place name.
nunatak	NU-na-tak	A mountaintop without any ice that sticks out of the ice cap.
qajait	ka-YA-it	Kayaks.
qajaq	QA-yaq	Kayak.
qivittut	qi-VIT-tut	Hermits who lived in the mountains.
Simiutaq	si-MIU-taq	Place name.
Siorartooq	sio-rar-TOOQ	Place name.
Talorsuit	ta-LOR-SUIT	Place name.

tooq	TOOQ	A tool for piercing sea ice so you can catch fish and seals in the winter.
tupilak	TU-pi-lak	Originally this word meant "ancestor's soul." In the old days, it was a figure with magical powers that you could use to hurt your enemy. Today they are used for decoration and souvenirs, and are often carved from narwhal tusk or caribou antlers.
ulu	OO-lu	A crescent knife traditionally used by women.
uluga	u-LU-ga	My ulu.
umiak	u-MIAK	Two umiaq.
umiat	u-MIAT	More than two umiaq.
umiaq	u-MIAQ	A large boat made from driftwood and covered in sealskin, made waterproof with blubber.

Maktaaq

INHABIT
MEDIA

IQALUIT • TORONTO

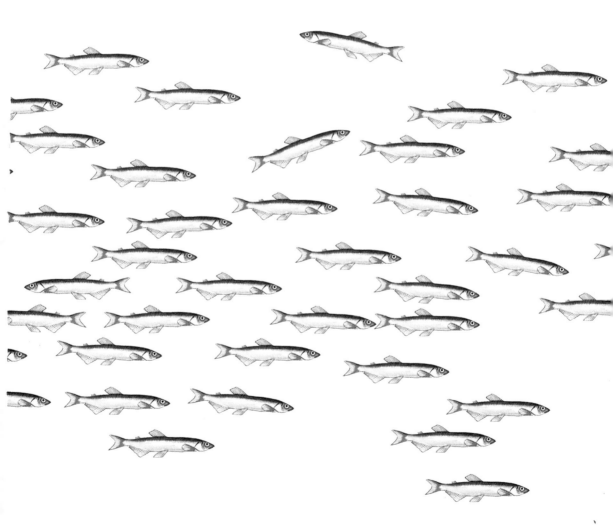